WHISKEY DEVILS

BRANDON ZENNER

Cover Design: James goonwrite.com
Formatting: Polgarus Studio PolgarusStudio.com

ISBN-13: 978-0692172797
ISBN-10: 0692172793

Library of Congress Control Number: 2018909465

Dedicated to my daughter, Sadie-Mae Zenner,
Your naptimes may have allowed me to finish this novel,
But it's the time when you're awake that inspires me the most.
I love you like crazy.

Chapter 1

Weaving through the crowd, I passed my exhausted coworkers, their faces gaunt and ghostly pale in the fluorescent lighting. All of them were salivating before the punch-out clock like a pack of ravenous hounds eager to tear into the flesh of that Friday night. They leaned from one leg to the other, purses in hand, sunglasses dangling from open collars. The din of conversation lessened as I neared the clock, and all eyes were cast upon me.

They were thinking, *Is he really going to do it? Is Powers leaving early?*

The receptionist's sharp stare burned with scorn from behind her blonde bangs, but I ignored her gaze and approached the clock. My time card was in my hand, "Evan Powers" scribbled on top. The paper glided effortlessly through the punch-out machine, making a slight mechanical noise as it stamped out the time, 4:47. The clicking noise echoed in the now-silent room, and I hightailed it to the door, daring my eager coworkers to follow.

Warm air cloaked me in all its glory as I flung the door open. My flesh tingled—honest to God, tingled—like the sun was drawing out some poison from the office's artificial cold air.

As I crossed the parking lot toward my car, I resisted turning to look through the wall-length window of the manager's office. Kim would be staring up from a stack of papers on her desk, watching me in disbelief as she checked the time on her watch. No one left before the clock struck five. No one.

1

Yeah, I did it. I left early. But fuck it—I quit. So there was that.

The well-traveled engine of my Buick rumbled to life, sputtering out clouds of gray exhaust. I backed out, put the car in drive, and sped the hell out of there.

A cigar was waiting for me in the glove box, and I clamped it between my teeth as I loosened the collar of my button-up shirt.

I laughed out loud, feeling a bit like a madman who laughs alone at the world, thinking, *I'm free, you fuckers—I'm free!* A cloud of cigar smoke was sucked out the window, replaced by the clean springtime breeze.

Traffic was already forming on the highway, but I had managed to beat the mass of cars that would stretch on for miles only minutes after five o'clock. The landscape gradually changed to an immense array of blossoming trees and flat wilderness as I distanced myself from town, driving deeper into the heart of the New Jersey Pine Barrens. My housemate Nick and I rented a nice piece of property: three acres of trees and land, with many more acres of wilderness in every direction. Our nearest neighbor was old Mr. Patrick, or Grandpa, and we didn't cross paths with the man too often. We invited him over whenever we had parties, but Grandpa rarely showed up and never stayed for long. He was cool with us, but when our parties got going, and a handful of ragged hippies turned into twenty, thirty, forty, sixty—whatever—he would take off. Not before schooling us all in a game of horseshoes, of course, and drinking about a six-pack of beer. The man could put them away.

I drove past Grandpa's mailbox and our driveway soon appeared. Nick's work truck came into view as I pulled in, and way out in the back of the yard I spotted him standing beside our massive garden. Nick had been living in the rental house for fifteen years. Our good friend, Darin Long, had been a housemate with us for the past five years, but due to his mother discovering that she has cancer, he had moved back home to Montana. Now it was only the two of us, all alone in that low ranch in the middle of the woods.

Hippie Nick, he was sometimes called, or more recently, The Old Man. It was a term of endearment. The guy had lived through the cultural revolution of the '60s and '70s, which meant that for most of our friends, myself included, Nick Grady was the closest thing to a legitimate hippie that we would ever encounter. The guy followed the Dead, marched at civil rights protests, and did all that fun stuff that made him practically a sage in the eyes of my stoner friends.

I got out of the car and passed Nick's work van on the way to the house. The *G* and *R* in Grady Construction and Repair on the van's side were barely legible, faded with time.

Our front door was unlocked, and I went straight to the kitchen. We had a strict nonsmoking rule indoors, for everything other than herb, so I had to be quick with my still-burning cigar. I grabbed two beers from the fridge and went out the kitchen door to the backyard. Nick was under the apple tree next to the garden, swaying with a beer in hand. The Dead blared from his portable CD player, the extension cord trailing all the way back to the house, lost like a snake in the grass.

Water droplets rained down from the sprinkler over the budding tomato plants, zucchinis, peppers, and everything else we'd planted only a few weeks ago. The corn stalks were already about two feet tall.

Nick moved to the music, barefoot, with his wrapped hemp necklaces and beadwork bouncing on his gray-haired chest. The only article of clothing the guy ever wore at home was a pair of cutoff jean shorts. When he saw me approaching he nodded.

"Hey there," I said.

Nick smiled a crooked smile, a rubber band stuck between his lips as he pulled his long hair out of his face. A cooler was out there next to the few battered Adirondack chairs, and I could tell by the look in Nick's eyes that he was already a few beers in. I handed him the beer I had brought from the kitchen anyway. Sierra Nevada, always Sierra Nevada. It was the only beer the guy would drink if given a choice. However, if he didn't have a choice, he'd drink most anything. Especially bourbon. We went through the stuff like it was water.

The song ended and he yelled out, "Yo, Powers! What's up, man?" He was evidently in a great mood.

"Nothing, Nick." I tried to be nonchalant, but my lips cracked into a smile. "I did it."

His eyes lit up. "You quit?"

I nodded.

"Ha!" He bounced over on quick feet and hugged me with his strong, skinny arms. "I'm so happy for you, brother. I know that job was dragging you down."

"Thanks, man."

"Want to call some people up, get the bonfire going?"

I shrugged. "I wouldn't mind having a few beers."

His face was radiant, and I knew he was swallowing back the question he'd been asking me for years now. The words were trying to burst free from his mouth, but I was going to wait a little while longer before letting him know that I would work for him full time. And I wasn't talking about his handyman service; as good as he was at repairing cabinets, replacing shingles, and even doing some landscaping for a handful of local Pineys. I was talking about his *other* job. His real job.

"You doing some shooting?" I nodded toward the small arsenal on the coffee table: his old Western-style six-shooters. They were a hobby of sorts, first for him, and then for me. After all, we did live in the middle of the woods. Not to mention that the house one over from old Mr. Grandpa's was the fire chief's, and the man was a regular at our parties—as clean-cut as he was—and he kept an eye on the police radio for call-ins about noise. I consider myself clean-cut as well, in comparison to most of the transients who pass through our doors. My hair is short, I wear nice pants and shirts, and I keep myself in decent shape. Ever since I met Nick, I've been trying to get the guy to go running with me, or use the weight bench in the basement. But he always declines. "Look at me," he says. "I'm skinny enough. There won't be nothing left of me." It's true. The guy's a rail: skinny and strong. A lifetime's worth of hard labor made it impossible for him to ever be a pound overweight.

Nick looked to the black powder pistols. "Knock yourself out," he said, and went back to swaying with the music, mumbling along with the words while looking out over the sea of vegetables glistening from the sprinkler water.

As the sun began to set and the beer in the cooler dwindled, we loaded and fired the six-shooters at a wide tree stump across the yard. The process of loading a black powder revolver was tedious, but that made shooting them all the more enjoyable. We had to work for our fun.

While we were shooting, the house phone rang several times, and soon our driveway became illuminated by headlights. A few people showed up with more beer, weed, and various low-grade narcotics and hallucinogens. Ritalin, Adderall—that sort of thing. Most everyone, myself excepted, got stoned the minute they crossed onto our property. Weed was never my thing. I rarely smoked, which was in contrast to the company I kept.

This guy named Mario showed up tripping on mushrooms, sitting a foot away from the blazing flames in the fire pit, his bright orange hair seeming to glow in the flickering light. I thought about asking him for a few caps, but decided against it. Ever since Darin moved out, Nick and I had to be on the lookout for people fucked up on the more serious drugs, like cocaine, heroin, and even speed. That was a big no-no at our home. Darin used to be our enforcer of sorts. He was a strong guy, although his short and stout build made him appear youthful, especially with his long dark hair kept up in a ponytail. Ex Army, believe it or not. But that life wasn't for him. Darin was a feel-good stoner who liked lounging around the house shirtless, just like Nick.

But Darin was gone, so it was up to Nick and me to watch over our guests. Just last party I found a guy taking a line of coke in our bathroom. He was so strung out that he forgot to lock the handle, and when I told him to get rid of the shit he started spewing vulgarities at me through his clattering jaw. Before his erratic mind thought it was a good idea to throw a swing, Nick and I had his arms behind his back, and we did the old heave-ho out the door, holding the back of his belt and his collar. I learned long ago in my bartending days to never let the other guy swing first. Unless of course the other guy was so fucked up that he couldn't hit the side of a wall. Or if the guy was a lawyer. Never hit a lawyer first. But back at my old bar, the local clientele were far from lawyers.

Lucky for us, the crowd was mellow tonight as the alcohol and marijuana flowed. At some point the fire chief showed up, wearing a big grin. He disappeared with Nick inside the house, and when he came back out, he was baked out of his mind.

"Hey, Powers," he said, his red eyes sparkling.

"What's up?"

"Check this out."

The fire chief swung a canvas duffel bag around from his shoulder and opened the zipper. A copious amount of fireworks lay inside.

"Cool, huh?"

"Yeah." I smiled. "Cool."

The night wore on and the fireworks were ignited to thunderous ovation from the enamored crowd. The fire chief kept his radio turned up in case the noise got called into the cops.

Maybe fifteen people were gathered in the backyard when I saw headlights approach from down the driveway and stop short of the house. I checked the time on my watch. It was impossible to see in the darkness, but I knew the headlights belonged to the black Plymouth Fury Gran Coupe that had been arriving at our house at that same time every week, for years now. I looked for Nick in the crowd and spotted him by the fire.

"Hey," I said, approaching.

When Nick looked at me, I tapped my watch and nodded toward the car. His face soured.

"Motherfucker," he muttered, and swilled back his beer.

Nick went to the house, and a moment later he emerged from the front, walking toward the car. He opened the passenger door, illuminating the car's interior while stepping inside.

It wasn't long until the passenger door opened again and Nick got out. The Plymouth reversed out of the driveway, not bothering to swing around the circle. Nick had told me in the past that the man didn't like it when strangers were at our house during his stops. But then he had gone on, "If he makes his stops on a Friday, it can't be avoided. Fuck him."

When Nick got close, I handed him a beer. His face was set in the same crazed anger that always overtook him after leaving the man in the Plymouth. I silently prayed that he wouldn't start hitting the bottle hard, like he often did after the man's visits, and go off on one of his insane rambles. Not now, not tonight. Tonight, I was celebrating my new life. My new path, as twisted as it might become.

"You okay?" I asked.

Nick took the beer and our eyes met. His face softened. "Yeah, man." He patted me on the shoulder, and we walked into the yard to join the circle of people watching the fire chief light off the last of his fireworks.

And there was Becka. Her fair complexion illuminated in bouncing shadows from the fire, her dark, somewhat curly hair pure black in the night.

"Hey," I said, walking up to her. "When'd you get here?"

She turned and smiled at the sound of my voice. "Hey, Powers. Just a minute ago. I was looking for you."

She patted the grass beside her and I took a seat, making it a point for our thighs to touch.

"I did it," I told her. "I quit."

"The office?"

"The office."

"Powers," she exclaimed. "That's wonderful, man!"

She reached over and wrapped her arms around me, burying her face in my chest.

This was good. This is what I needed. I needed Becka, her arms holding me tight all night long. When was the last time we'd hooked up? A week ago? Maybe more. Nick jokingly referred to Becka as my girlfriend, but we were nothing like that. Just friends. Two people in their mid-thirties who had been in terrible relationships, much like all the other loners out there who find themselves still single past their twenties. We just wanted to keep things cool. Sure, we liked each other, but we didn't want to make our relationship something more than it needed to be. For her birthday last year I bought her a small oval locket. Nothing fancy or expensive. I regretted giving it to her the moment I saw the surprise and uncertainty on her face. She did wear it, though, up until recently. She said she misplaced it, put it down somewhere, and that it's got to be around. Probably at home. Probably fell from the kitchen sink. She'd find it, she told me.

But who knows.

Becka had been friends with Nick for years longer than I'd known either of them. I originally thought that Nick and Becka had a romantic past, but

Darin later set me straight. Besides, their ages are decades apart … not that that would stop either of them.

As the last explosion filled the air, the fire chief turned to the crowd. "That's it," he said, displaying his empty duffel bag. "That's all she wrote."

Nick stood a few feet away from the crowd and we caught each other's eyes.

"Hey, Becka, you gonna be here for a few minutes?"

She looked up at me with a smile and then back to the fire. "I'm not going anywhere."

I hugged her shoulder and stood. "Be right back."

"Hey, grab me a beer while you're at it?" She displayed her near-empty bottle, the light from the fire making it transparent.

"Of course." I smiled, walking toward Nick. "Be right back."

Nick and I stood apart from the group as the fire chief shook out a few stray firecrackers into the fire, turning the duffel bag upside down and shaking it out.

"Hey," Nick shouted over the roar of our friends laughing and jumping away from this madman dumping explosives over the open flame. "We gotta talk."

"Yeah," I said. "I know."

"You give my proposition some thought?"

I nodded, not that he could see me with his eyes transfixed on the fire. With Darin gone, Nick was shorthanded. He'd been asking me to work full time at his operation for years, but I always declined. I was too clean-cut for that life, I used to think. I was better off as a part-time employee. But after spending three years stuck at a cubicle in the stalest environment that I could possibly imagine, wasting away the best and most productive time of the day—between nine and five, when the human mind and body is at its best— I was starting to see things in a different light. Plus, he was offering me more than just hours—he was offering me a management position. Small responsibilities at first, but they would grow over time. But the real benefit, I thought, was that Becka and I would be spending more time together.

"Yeah, Nick, I've given your proposition a lot of thought. I'm in. I'm all aboard."

He turned to me. "Seriously?"

"Seriously."

He extended a hand, smiling like a little boy. "Oh, brother, you are most needed!"

We shook, and then of course he hugged me.

"Man, this is going to be great!" he shouted, arms out in the air, holding his beer aloft to the night sky. The light from the fire flickered dancing shadows all over his body.

"We'll start tomorrow," he said, taking a swig of beer and bouncing on his toes.

I smiled.

He tossed the empty straight into the roaring flame, and grabbed two cold ones from the cooler. He popped the caps and handed me a bottle.

"Cheers, brother," he said.

We clinked glasses.

"Cheers."

He took a long pull, and I again prayed to myself that he wouldn't get too fucked up. I didn't need him screaming crazy shit at our guests, crying, sobbing, and making no sense at all.

"I think it will be best if we start late," he said after a burp.

"Agreed."

Sipping my beer, I watched Becka transfixed on the fire, a smile on her radiant face as she swayed to the music. As much of a free spirit as she was, Becka had something about her. She had class, and an amazing mind that I wanted to keep discovering. She wasn't the type of person to lay her cards out on the table; I had to keep guessing what was in her hand. Her beauty was the type that tongue-tied men, but there was more between us than sheer attraction. We had a chemistry that couldn't be put into words, but only felt as a throbbing heat in my chest. It was intrigue that kept me coming back for more; it was her quiet, pondering eyes that displayed indecipherable emotion. Simple words from her lips carried the weight of the world and affected me like I imagine poetry inspires minds greater than my own.

Her shadowy form beckoned me to approach and sit with her on that lush field of grass for as long as eternity would allow.

Turning, I grabbed two beers from the cooler. I was about to tell Nick that I would be back, but he had seen the rapture in my eyes and had begun to drift away, chatting with the fire chief.

"Welcome back," Becka said, looking up to me as I approached. There was longing in her eyes.

Feeling a bit drunk, I smiled coolly and took a seat beside her to watch the roaring bonfire.

Tomorrow, my life would change—for the better, I thought. I would be managing a productive and quite illegal drug operation. But now, in the present moment, I didn't want to contemplate the future or lament the past. I wanted to stay stuck in time, right where I was.

Chapter 2

My head was spinning. The last time I looked at the clock it said two a.m. and Becka was giving me a goodbye kiss. Now, 10:45 a.m. blazed from the clock. I desperately wanted to sleep the day away, but there were two things that were driving me out of the bed:

1. I had to pee, excruciatingly bad.
2. I needed the largest and coldest glass of water that was possible.

Nick's room was on the way to the bathroom, and his door was wide open. The bright sun shone through the American flag that he used as a curtain along with the dozen or so blue glass bottles that lined his windowsill, casting the room in varying shades of red and blue. Those colors in the morning had a strange effect on me that I wasn't sure if I liked. They were somehow both agitating and soothing.

After my morning pee that seemed to never end, I stuck my head into Nick's room, expecting to see him passed out on top of his blankets, still in his cutoff shorts.

But he wasn't there.

As I walked into the kitchen the back door flew open, and in came Nick bouncing on his toes, holding a tall glass of something red with a green sprout sticking out.

"Hey, Powers, you're up!"

He was wide awake, apparently.

I rubbed my eyes. "When'd you get up?"

He shrugged. "About an hour ago."

The kitchen smelled of coffee, which was most welcoming. I poured myself a tall glass of water and a mug full of hot, black coffee and sat at the table.

"This is what you need, man, if you want to fly right." Nick opened the refrigerator.

"A Bloody Mary?" I was going to dismiss the idea of drinking anything alcoholic, but I had to admit, it sounded appealing.

Nick made a drink and put it on the table before me. He then went to the cabinet to remove two aspirin from the container, along with either a Ritalin or Adderall leftover from a party, placing them all next to my drink. Then he went to the stove to scramble some eggs.

"You're in a good mood," I said, looking down at my variety of drinks and pills.

"Damn straight." He cracked eggs into a bowl.

Watching him at the stove, a flashback from last night passed through my memory: I saw Nick get in one of his dreaded drunken moods, crawling across the grass in inebriated delirium. It must have been around the time everyone left and my memory was becoming fuzzy. He was shouting the same fragmented statements, things he only ever brought up at the tail end of a serious bender. But he always cut himself short of fully explaining what he was talking about. He spoke as if battling some demon inside him, so all I would get was "It's—they ... they's took me, man—it was *them*. I only, didn't want to do it, man," and he would be crying. "I-I was a just a k-kid, man, those fucking-fucks, they-they took me, man!" Whatever he was talking about, I wasn't sure that I wanted to know. Occasionally, he would shout the same jumbled utterances while sleeping. I was warned a long time ago to never wake him up if I heard screaming in the middle of the night. So I never did. Darin had known Nick way longer than I had, so he was able to wake him out of those episodes without getting himself killed.

Nick put a plate of eggs before me along with a bottle of hot sauce.

"Eat up," he said. "Then go take a shower. We're leaving in half an hour."

I nodded. I knew I had made an agreement, but I'd been half expecting Nick to be just as hungover as myself. Unfortunately, he wasn't.

***

We took Nick's van to the highway, and then drove south for about twenty minutes. He was taking me to two locations, both of which I had already seen. One was his office, since I was now expected to help keep tabs on the books. The building itself was tiny, an old one-car garage, the sliding door patched up with drywall and converted into a single office room with a bathroom in the back. A battered wooden sign read "Grady Construction and Repair" over the front door.

It was a *mess*.

Papers everywhere, filing cabinets overflowing with files, and Nick's blue glass jars and bottles bordering every spare inch around the room's two windows. On top of the cabinets was an assortment of rocks and crystals.

Nick read the expression on my face. "Don't worry about all this." His hands danced over the room. "We can clean up however you like. This," he said, pointing to the corner of the room, "is where we keep the important stuff." He grabbed the sides of a filing cabinet and slid it aside. Then he knelt down, feeling the edge of a strip of molding. He pulled, and the baseboard came free of the magnets keeping it in place. Nick put the molding aside, and reached into a cavity to remove several large ledgers, placing them each on the desk in turn.

"These are the books," he said. "Expense reports. Payroll. A section of the wall pops free too. That's where we hide the safe."

"How are the books standing?" The random slips of papers jutting out from the pages answered my question. A few even fell out and drifted to the floor.

"Well," Nick said, scratching the side of his face, "not as bad as they look, but I'm close to falling behind. I'm juggling too much at the moment."

I nodded.

"All right then." I started rolling up my sleeves. "Should we start?"

"Not yet." Nick shook his head. "We're going to the warehouse first. With Darin gone, I'm still shorthanded at the operation. I want to show you a few things. That's where you'll be needed the most."

We had previously negotiated a salary on the way to the office, and had

13

settled on a fair rate—more than fair. About twice of what cubicle hell was paying me. I would do whatever was needed. There was no way I was going to fuck this up; it wasn't like I could bounce around from job to job forever. This was it.

Nick put the ledgers back in the hole in the wall, replaced the molding, and moved the cabinet back in place. The little shiny rocks jittered on top.

Then he turned to the door, and I followed him out.

We drove to another part of town, closer to the shore. The area was industrial, with large warehouses belonging to FedEx and UPS, as well as about a dozen or so smaller companies. Nick drove across a vast and vacant paved lot and parked around the corner of a windowless rectangular building, all steel and metal. The wall approaching had a large faded mural of graffiti, which must have been vibrant, perhaps even nice when it was first spray painted by whatever talented kids vandalized it. The graffiti had been painted over with a nearly transparent coating of white paint, but the colors showed through. This was the first time I was seeing it this early in the day, and the rainbow, cartoonish mural of a girl's face along with some zigzag signatures were legible.

Nick parked next to a white sedan with several moving vans nearby. A dark blue Mercedes-Benz sat a few spots down. The car was a little beat-up, but still looked sharp.

My part-time work for Nick had always been late at night when the other workers were long gone. It was Nick's design that not all of his employees should meet and know each other. A good business model when you're in his type of trade. The only people I ever worked with in those long dark hours were Becka and a security guard named Jeff. But that guy didn't talk much, just drank coffee and watched old movies on his portable television. That's how I got to know Becka: at the warehouse. She'd been working for Nick … I don't know, maybe seven years longer than myself? Maybe more.

Nick got out, and I followed him to a side door. Earlier, he had given me his master code. I still had my own code, but along with my promotion came the responsibility of increased knowledge. Only myself, Nick, and one other employee had the master code. Nick entered it on a keypad and a little LED flashed from red to green. Inside, a large man stood up from a folding chair holding a crumpled crossword puzzle and a pencil.

"Nick," the man said, nodding.

"Mark, brother, meet Powers."

The day-shift guard named Mark reached out and shook my hand. He stood a foot taller than the both of us, and his palm looked like an elephant stump coming out of his black leather jacket.

"My pleasure," I said.

"Same."

"That your Benz out there?"

He nodded.

"Nice car."

"Thanks." He sat back down, his attention going to the folded newspaper. "I'm looking to trade it in. You in the market, let me know."

We walked directly across the hall, to a second door leading to a second warehouse. It was like those Russian matryoshka dolls that get pulled apart to reveal smaller dolls nesting inside. A warehouse within a warehouse.

Nick took me to the door and knocked.

My previous work took place down the long hall to the left, in a room around the corner in the rear of the building, and I looked over my shoulder to where I normally worked with Becka. She was nowhere to be seen. Whatever Nick was about to show me was new, but I had a good idea of *exactly* what was behind that thick door.

A sliding viewing port opened, and a set of eyes looked out. The viewing port closed, and the sound of a heavy lock clacked from the hollows of the metal door. A moment later it opened and we stepped inside, shielding our eyes from the glaring light.

"Holy hell," I muttered, stepping into the room. The temperature was hot in there, muggy, and my eyes were practically blinded from the succession of thousand-watt high-pressure sodium lightbulbs lining the ceiling. A sea of tall marijuana plants filled the room, all set in arranged rows, some attached to an elaborate hydroponic system. The smell of fresh marijuana was as thick as soup. A silver tray holding orange slices and a knife sat on a table by the door.

"So." I turned to Nick. "What exactly do you need me to do?"

Nick scratched the side of his temple. "A little bit of everything. We need a hand in the grow room here, that's for sure. You'll still be needed in the back, cutting, drying, and packaging the plants, like you've been doing. Maybe one day you'll be doing deliveries, but we'll see about that when the time comes."

"Okay," I said, nodding. This was a lot to take in, but I was happy to hear that my night shifts with Becka were still in the picture. We were approaching our monthly custom of having a quickie on the break-room table.

I was daydreaming of Becka's silky thighs rubbing against my ribcage, wrapped around the small of my back, when Nick said, "Hey man, you look stressed. Don't worry."

He patted me on the shoulder, then picked up two orange slices from the silver plate, handing me one. "It's good luck," he said, tearing the juicy flesh from the rind. "Eat one coming in and one going out." He tossed the rind in a drum of half-decomposed mulch.

The tangy juice rushed into my mouth.

"It will be the same as hanging out in our garden," he said. "Trust me."

Chapter 3

Nick's two black powder pistols were laid out on the table. One was a reproduction 1857 Colt Walker with blackened metal and dark wood grips. The other was a reproduction 1858 Remington New Army: stainless steel with similar dark wood grips. They were both bulky old six-shooters, top of the line back in the mid-1800s.

Guns weren't something I had been into before meeting Nick—but damn, shooting those things sure was fun. Each pistol was as long as my forearm, and they bucked strong when fired.

Nick and I filled the guns' chambers with powder and rammed the balls behind. We were getting ready to put a few more targets out on the stump when I asked him, "So, who is he?"

"Who's who?" Nick was applying a layer of grease over each chamber of the rotating ammunition cylinder to prevent a chain fire—when the flame or spark of firing one bullet spreads to others in the neighboring chambers.

"The guy on payroll. Is he the same guy in the Plymouth?"

Nick's expression went sour.

"Look," I said, softening my tone. "You have me sorting payroll, so I think it's safe to assume—"

"He's my partner, okay?" Nick blurted out, concentrating on placing the firing caps firmly on the guns' cylinders.

I felt stupid for even bringing it up. I wasn't planning on it, but after the third beer the words sort of slipped past my lips. Part of my job was to write down the staff's hourly figures from the time cards into the ledger, then pass them over to Nick so he could stuff the envelopes with cash. An entire half of the business's proceeds went straight to someone named Carpenter X. I had been writing down his figures for the past month and a half since I started working full time. Yet this guy, Mr. Carpenter X, never stepped foot on the property. Not that I was aware of.

There were four security guards working in revolving shifts, Nick, of course, and one other botanist named Jim Hoffman, who was management as well. Jim sort of looked like Nick, maybe a few years younger, but with a great big beard. He was another product of the revolutionary baby boomers. A bit wild, and a friend of Nick's since they were kids. The guy bounced around the garden of marijuana, dancing from one plant to the other, always with his portable CD player plugged in his ears. His large wire-frame glasses were constantly sliding down his nose, which would get real annoying when working with the guy for hours on end. All he had to do was tighten the nose pads. I wanted to yell, "Jim, fix those fucking things already!"

"All right," I said, placing the last firing cap on my pistol. "Just wondering. No worries. Forget it."

"Look." Nick sighed. "Don't worry about him, okay? We've had an arrangement since before you were born. I deal with him—nobody else talks to the man."

His voice was testy.

I changed the subject.

"Want to set up the targets?" I asked.

"Sure as shit."

We placed a few overripe tomatoes that had fallen off the vine on the stump, along with a number of tin cans that were riddled with bullet holes.

Standing side by side, we took a moment to polish off our beers. When Nick finished, he tossed his bottle aside with a belch. I asked him, "Ready?"

"Damn straight," he replied, wiping his mouth.

I faced the targets, my pistol in the thigh-hugging holster. Nick did the same.

"Okay ... three ... two ... one ... *fire!*"

We drew and fired, which was not all that quick considering we were shooting black powder revolvers made for the Old West. But we were decent shots with them, and our speed had improved remarkably over the years. Nick in particular could fire each round almost as fast as an automatic. The hours we'd spent getting drunk and shooting those pistols while listening to Nick's CD player were staggering. When the smoke cleared, only one tomato remained intact.

We sat in our Adirondack chairs, letting the pistols cool before cleaning and rearming them. Nick popped the caps off two more beers and handed me one.

"Look," he said, "about my partner—"

"Hey, I get it," I cut in. "It's none of my business. I'm sorry that I brought it up."

"It's a long story." He paused, put his beer in the grass, and grabbed the handle of Jack Daniels, taking a swig from the rim. He made an unpleasant face and passed the bottle.

"I don't have a choice." He shook his head as if losing his train of thought, his mind off in some distant memory.

"What's that?"

"A choice. I don't have a choice. I … have to work with him, and that's final."

This was news to me, and I was starting to get the feeling that whatever the story was with Carpenter X, it really wasn't any of my business. I always thought that Nick was solely in charge of the operation. It was his business, his plants, his contacts, his distribution channels. Jim Hoffman was his equal in horticultural ability alone. Despite all the time I spent living and working with Nick, I had never known the extent of his operation. He'd never talked openly about it, which—in my opinion—made him a *good* drug dealer. The scope of his business was still a surprise to me, even though I spent countless hours packaging ample amounts of his product in the back room of the warehouse.

The evening wore on, and we stopped talking about work. We loaded and fired our pistols until it got too dark to see the stump. Then we watered the garden and turned off the hose. Nick was hitting the bottle hard as we sat under the apple tree. I got up to pee in the grass and when I came back, Nick was holding the bottle of whiskey in wobbly hands, trying to focus on taking another swig.

He blurted out, "Fuck-fucks'ers w-won't lets me leave …"

"What?"

"Fucking guy …"

His voice had that crackle. The whiskey was releasing Nick's suppressed demons and splintering his words into insane babble.

To be honest, I really wasn't in the mood. I just wanted to get drunk and maybe order a pizza. Dealing with one of Nick's tearful introspections over something he wouldn't tell me about was not how I wanted to spend the evening. Not to mention the constant need for me to be saying things like, "It's okay, man. It's okay," when I had no clue what I was okaying.

So I said, "Hmm."

Nick managed another swig. He coughed, sputtered, and said, "I c-can't gets out. The fuckers took me, they t-took me. I-I's only a kid." The tears were coming. "T-t-they got what t-they deserves, those fucks! *Those fucks!*" He started yelling, I mean, loud, "Those fucking fuckers! I's was only a kid!" He got up and staggered, but then he stood and threw the half-finished bottle of whiskey into the darkness. It hit the grass and bounced over the lawn.

"Who, Nick? Who?" I was startled to see him this riled up. It was rare for his emotional outpouring to turn violent, and it was a bit frightening.

He stood straight, his knees shaking, and he lifted his pistol.

"They's only o-one left."

He pulled the trigger and the sound of the shot nearly caused me to jump out of my seat.

"Jesus!" I didn't know he had reloaded his gun. I thought we were done shooting for the night.

He pulled the trigger again and again, wildly missing the bottle in the lawn. Tears were running down his face and he was spitting up strings of spittle as he screamed, "I'll get you! I'll g-get you! You're the last one, and I'll fucking *kill* you!"

When the pistol clicked empty and his screams subsided, my startled mind told me to do something. But I was scared shitless. Nick was so drunk that I didn't think he could differentiate between me and the bottle of bourbon on the lawn. He stood there in the silence, pulling the trigger on empty chambers. And then he stopped. His arm fell slack and he went to step forwards, but he just sort of stumbled in place and collapsed on his knees. Then he fell over on his back. I had never seen him so drunk. His sobbing became quieter and quieter as he now lay on his side.

"You—you okay, man?"

He didn't respond, but made a light moaning sound.

I sat there in silence for what seemed like an eternity, not moving from my chair. Soon, I heard the gentle sound of deep breathing. He was fast asleep.

I sighed. Now feeling entirely sober, I carefully took the pistol out of his hand. In the darkness, I gathered up the other pistol and all the accessories, and took everything to the house. I came back with a blanket and tossed it over Nick, and then just stood there looking down at the old man. What the hell was he talking about? Christ, I was hoping that he wouldn't remember any of this in the morning, because I honestly didn't want to have a conversation about it.

The moonlight cast a glow over the grass in the lawn, and the bright reflection of the whiskey bottle shone out like a lighthouse beckoning a lost ship at sea. I retrieved the bottle and took a long swig, and my face contorted in that just-drank-whiskey face. Then I turned and went inside.

Chapter 4

A few weeks passed, and I was really getting the hang of the job. Nick was right: tending to the abundance of crops was just like hanging out in the garden. The only difference was that I was entirely more sober while doing it, and the job was a bit more technical. In the vegetable garden, we only occasionally checked the pH levels and fertilized when needed. For the crops in the warehouse, making sure the NPK nutrients—nitrogen, phosphorus, and potassium—were added to the soil was a necessity.

We used an assortment of fertilizers, but the brands changed so often that it was hard to keep up. That was Jim's job anyway. He selectively purchased organic fertilizers or concocted them himself. The guy was a wizard, mixing together different compounds, testing and retesting the levels until they were just right. I never saw the guy without his PPM pen—parts per million— hanging out his back pocket. He was constantly sticking the thing, which looked like a souped-up electric thermometer, in the soil, fussing over the salt content and the amount of dissolved solids. We had various plants in various stages of life, and both a hydroponic system and rows of plants in good old-fashioned dirt. Jim was responsible for mixing all the soil and labeling the various fertilizers to correspond to the life cycle of the plants.

In a way, I was sort of Jim's apprentice while I worked with him— although you wouldn't know it, since the guy rarely took out his headphones to explain what he was doing. But he always made sure I was watching when he prepared soils or mixed nitrogen-laden organic compounds in the mulch piles. Some of it I knew, like adding coffee grounds, but being certain not to add too much because of the acidity.

Jim's main thing was earthworms—the guy loved them. Probably kept them as pets. He would come into the warehouse carrying buckets of dark brown soil smelling strongly of shit, with plump, thick worms wriggling around all throughout. He would say with a smile, "Got a friend over on the horse farm, the worms love the soil there. She gives me this stuff for a few joints. Just a few joints! Gold," he would say. "Gold."

I was seeing a bit much of Jim lately.

Unfortunately, I wasn't seeing Becka much more than I used to, which was a real shame. But we were still able to have our monthly session on the break-room table, which was a plus.

She was interested in my new job, a bit jealous even, I thought. She would say stuff like, "Looks like you're my new boss," with a pouty smirk, and I would reply, "You wish."

It was kind of a turn-on when she would say stuff like that during sex, calling me her boss, but it was hard to tell if she was joking around or if she was generally upset that I had taken on more responsibilities. We never talked about it, but the girl had been working for Nick much longer than myself. Not only that, but she was responsible for curing our primo product. The expensive stuff. Those plants would get cut down, dried and clipped, and then placed in glass jars, ranging in size from Mason jars to gallon containers. The jars were sealed and then reopened often to let the product breathe. She would go from jar to jar, examining the buds and sniffing the inside like a wine connoisseur, all the while jotting down notes in her spiral notebook. It could take weeks to months until the product was properly cured, and it was Becka's job to be certain that the buds reached their peak in flavor and potency. When they were done and Becka deemed her product had reached its greatest potential, I could smell it from the door of the packaging room like thick perfume. The buds would be sticky and dense, and no two looked alike.

Although I wasn't a smoker myself, I did have an admiration for the beauty of the stuff. There was something enticing about the buds, the range of colors and the sweet fragrances. When I looked up close, there was much more to see than just a plain green plant. The buds had patches of purples and red, with fiery orange hairs, and they were all covered in a mist of fine crystals, like sugar. Those crystals were a mark of the product's strength. The more crystals, the better the high.

I loved working with Becka on the jars. It was fun watching her forehead furrow while sniffing the air to determine if the batch was at its peak. Lately, though, she had stopped explaining to me her process, the smells and ripeness she was looking for—the subtle nuances in the aroma and dryness that determined her method. Maybe her way of getting back at me for getting a promotion was giving me the cold shoulder.

As well as Becka and I had gotten to know each other over the years, we still never discussed our feelings about the job—which is kind of a good mindset to have when dealing with illegal drugs. Airing grievances, even with the people closest to us, can have unfortunate consequences. Maybe she wanted my job, more responsibility, better pay? Who knows? And I wasn't about to start asking. None of my business. I was happy to keep my relationship with Becka strictly to friendship, occasional sex, and maybe a dinner out once in a while. Two people having fun.

I didn't know why Nick had offered me the job and not her, but I had a number of guesses—one of them being that I could make things grow. Not that I was a professional, compared to Nick or Jim, but I loved spending time out in the garden, tending to the plants and watching things come alive and thrive. I loved the feeling of good clean soil on my hands, caked in the folds of my fingers and under my nails. I enjoyed seeing the difference one fertilizer could make over another. Gardening got me high in a way. It cleared my mind, flushed the stress out of my body. And like I said, I had a knack for the job. Just look at last year's vegetable harvest, the dozens of bright red tomatoes bursting with juices. Zucchinis and cucumbers so plump and crisp that they were best eaten raw with just a sprinkle of sea salt. And I did it all without the aid of pesticides or chemicals.

At the warehouse, our product was sometimes picked up when the crop was ready, but usually Nick delivered it with Jim. I think it was his way of looking out for me, to make sure I wasn't around for the exchanges. I never saw the product leave or money exchange hands. The shipment room was always cleared when I arrived in the mornings.

Making deliveries was the last chain in the link to upper management, and Nick himself had to deem me worthy.

Chapter 5

A few days later, I was mixing a fertilizer labeled 1-10-2—the NPK ratio—in a pail of water with Jim working beside me, the guy constantly checking that I was using the right combination of fertilizer to coincide with the life stage of the plants.

"You're not using the ten-o-six, are you?" His voice was congested, his words coming out thick.

I wiped the sweat off my forehead with my forearm, feeling the granules of dirt grind against my skin as I looked up at him. I moved the bucket so he could see the label.

"All right," he said, "all right," and plugged his earphones back in.

The guy was sick—flu sick. His moves were off, and he wasn't humming and singing along to his inaudible music. His nose was raw and his eyes were bloodshot. The guy looked miserable.

He really didn't have to be there. I was perfectly capable of handling the plants until he got better. But Jim was a workaholic and a perfectionist—his plants were his obsession, his life, his family and children. Being away from them was difficult.

He had started getting sick a few days earlier, when he asked me to help him pick up some soil.

"It's my back," he'd said. "Sore to the touch."

So we drove to the worm farm, as Jim called it, watching the scenery change from trees and brush to flat fields.

"Just look at that soil," he'd said, shaking his head. "So many worms. A sea of gold."

I rolled my eyes.

Jim got his soil from this skinny girl named Cheryl who worked out there in the service area of a majestic stable—although you wouldn't know its opulence by entering through the back roads like we had done. Just a field of dirt, with horses snorting and whinnying out by a water trough, their thick muscles rippling like coiled rope under their taut skin. Cheryl seemed a part of that landscape, like she'd been born of the soil. Her skin was weathered and raw, and her lanky body had been hardened by years of labor. She also didn't seem to bathe often, and didn't shave her legs, armpits, or anywhere else, I'd imagine.

Jim had gone off by the barn to smoke a joint with Cheryl, who was all too happy to take a break from her work. She smiled, brushing her long dreadlocks off her shoulders.

"You want a hit?" she asked as I returned to the barn to grab another pail of Jim's "golden" soil.

"Nah, I'm good."

Cheryl shrugged, and passed the joint to Jim.

A while back at a party, Cheryl got really stoned, and forgetting that Becka and I had a thing, said something along the lines of "Can't stand that bitch." So ever since then I'd rarely spoken to her.

I finished loading the van with the buckets of soil and went to find a cigar I'd left in the glove box. As I lit the end, rolling the tip over the flame, I spied in the side mirror Jim and Cheryl still talking by the barn. He handed her a baggie filled with rolled joints, which she pressed to her nose and seemed to savor. Then they hugged. And then they kissed.

My eyebrow rose.

"Jim, you old dog," I said under my breath. "Maybe it's not just the soil that keeps you coming back."

On our way home from the worm farm, I asked Jim, "So, what's Cheryl's deal with Becka anyway?"

"Not sure man, not sure. Don't really care to investigate any further, to tell ya the truth. Back in the day, Cheryl and Nick used to kick it once in a while."

27

I didn't mention that I'd just seen the two of them kiss.

Cheryl gets around, I thought.

Jim continued, "They had a thing kind of like you and Becka got now, maybe even less of a thing. They just hooked up here and there. You know how Nick is. The guy's a free spirit. He'd fuck just about anything that moves."

"You think him and Becka—"

"No, man. And it won't do your head any good thinking that way. Nick and Cheryl had a thing around the time Becka started hanging around. My guess, Cheryl was a bit jealous that some pretty young girl was floating around Nick's place. I don't think it's anything more than that. Cheryl just never liked her."

"Strange."

"Yeah, maybe." Jim shrugged. "Or maybe Cheryl's just a bitch."

He laughed, and so did I.

That was only a few days back, and since then, Jim's sore back had turned into a full-blown sickness.

"Oh man," he said in the warehouse, taking a break to blow his nose, which sounded like his sinuses exploding.

I moved to the next plant over, and said, "You should really take the day off."

"Can't do," he said. "Delivery tonight."

"Shit. Well ... I can go. If you're sick, that is."

"No, no." He shooed his hands dismissively. "I'm fine. I'll be okay."

A few hours later I said goodbye to Jim as he busied himself mixing the fertilizer for the hydroponic reservoir, and wished him well. He nodded, not removing his headphones. I took my slice of orange off the plate, ate it, and tossed the peel in the mulch pile. Outside, I was just starting up my car when I saw Nick pull in next to Jim's white sedan.

"Hey," I said, rolling down my window. "What's up?"

"Hey, Powers. What's up?"

"Nothing. Listen, Jim's real sick in there."

"What's that? He's sick?" Nick spoke, walking toward the door.

"Yeah, man. He doesn't look so hot."

Nick seemed unfazed.

"Hey," I said, trying to make eye contact. "You all right?"

"Me? Yeah, I'm good."

"Well," I continued, "if you want me to make his delivery, I can. You know—if he's sick."

"I'll keep that in mind." Nick tapped the hood of my car and took off toward the door.

"Hey," I shouted. "Want me to pick up some beer on my way home?"

He paused, his hand on the keypad. "Sure, man," he shouted back, then disappeared inside.

I put the car in reverse.

"What the fuck's up with him?"

Chapter 6

I picked up beer and drained a few in front of the TV while I waited for Nick to come home. About an hour into some old spaghetti Western the phone rang in the middle of a shoot-out between an outlaw and the townsfolk. I let it ring three times before I got off the couch, hoping that a commercial would pause the action.

"Shit," I muttered, running to the kitchen. I looked over my shoulder as I picked up the receiver. One of the townsfolk got shot off a rooftop and fell crashing down onto a carriage below, in the most dramatic fashion possible.

"Hello?" I said.

"Powers? That you?"

"Becka. Hey, what's up?"

"Nothing ... you all right?"

"What? Yeah, I'm fine."

"You sound out of breath. What's all that noise? Those gunshots?"

"It's nothing. Just the TV." I looked around for the remote, and could see it sitting on the couch cushion. I went to the back door, pulling the phone cord until it was taut, and closed the back door behind me.

Becka continued, "You working tonight?"

"Not tonight. I worked the day shift."

I thought I was about to get an earful of scorn; she'd be pissed that our shifts had changed. But she went on, "No bother. I have some time before I go in. You up for a quick beer?"

"Sure. I'm home if you want to stop by."

"All right, cool. See you in a few."

I went back inside and hung up, wanting to see how the shoot-out was going. But a commercial for fruit juice was flashing on the screen in mind-numbing bursts of color designed to catch the eye of children so they would urge their parents to buy whatever crap the marketers were force-feeding them.

While I waited for Becka, I nursed a beer and saw the better half of the old grainy movie. It didn't take long until she showed up, and I was getting up off the couch to let her in when she knocked once and then opened the door.

"Hey, Powers," she said with a smile, and then looked at what I was watching.

"Yeah, I know," I said. "I'll change it."

"No, no. It's no problem," she told me. But the smile was gone from her face. I've never met a woman who liked the old Westerns.

Once, I tried to explain to Becka, "If you just watch it, you'll see that it's good."

She answered, "It's for boys, Powers."

"Yeah, but ..."

"Powers—it's for boys."

That was it. Case closed.

I clicked off the television and got her a beer.

"I only have about an hour before I have to leave for work."

I looked at the time and nodded.

"Where's Nick?"

"No clue." I shrugged. "Should be home by now. Last I saw him he was hightailing it into the warehouse."

She nodded and sipped her beer. "Working late I suppose." She put her beer down and arranged herself on the couch, moving closer, our knees touching.

"So ... I only have an hour, Powers." She looked right in my eyes and held her gaze there.

That was all I needed. I put my beer down and moved in, eager to have her right there on the couch. We kissed heavily for several minutes, our clothing coming off, when she said, "Let's go to your room."

"We'll hear Nick's truck if he comes home."

"I want to go to your bed." She went to kiss me, the fragrant vanilla scent of her hair hitting my nostrils, but instead of a kiss she bit my lower lip just hard enough for me to feel some pain. Then she relented with a smile.

"All right, then." I grabbed her hand and pulled her toward my bedroom, and we fell on the mattress in a jumble.

Becka wanted to be on top, commanding, and I had no problem with that. Her hair was down, and when she leaned over to kiss me her bouncy strands surrounded my face, cutting out the faint hallway light. It was just me and her.

We had sex fast and intense, and when we'd finished she stayed by my side, resting her head on my chest. I buried my nose in the top of her hair and breathed in. Then I leaned up and looked at the time.

"Becka, you're going to be late."

Her head nodded against my chest, but she didn't get up.

"Just another minute," she whispered.

Her hand played over my chest hair, swirling it around, then patting it flat. A few minutes went by, and then she rolled over and moved to sit up. My chest where her head had lain was warm and ... wet?

Shit.

"Becka, what's the matter?" I felt the dampness with my hand and sat up, touching her shoulders.

"What?" She pulled away and stood, tying her hair up.

"What's wrong? Are you crying?"

She wouldn't face me as she got dressed.

"No." She shook her head, and I watched her rub her eyes on her shirt as she slid it over her face. Then she turned to me.

"You're a good guy, Powers."

It was happening again.

"Becka ..."

"You should have a girlfriend. A real one. Maybe a wife. Someone to come home to every night, not just a person like me who can't ..."

"Becka." I stood from the bed. "You know I'm happy. I would tell you if I wasn't."

This wasn't the first time we were having this little conversation. She'd explain that she was damaged goods, not girlfriend material, incapable of relationships, yada yada. I didn't agree, but at the same time, I wasn't looking for a relationship, so what we had going on was ideal.

"Seriously Becka, you can't go on thinking that something's wrong with you just because you've dated some fucked-up guys. You need to—"

She put a finger over my mouth and shook her head. "Okay, Powers. Okay. I'm sorry. Let's not end in a fight; I'm just emotional is all. I'm sorry. I'm just …" She smiled. "I'm happy, I am. I like you, Powers. You're a good man, and you deserve the best."

I was about to reply, but she grabbed me tight and hugged me close. A good, strong hug. When we parted she said, "I'm going to be late."

She finished getting dressed, and I walked her to the door. She turned and kissed me, holding my gaze an extra moment, and then she walked toward her car in the moonlight. I leaned against the doorframe until her taillights snaked out of view. The night was beautiful, with a warm breeze. I stood there in my underwear for several minutes, listening to the crickets.

Then I turned and closed the door, deciding that I needed one more beer before bed. By now the Western would be over, so I didn't bother turning the television back on.

In the kitchen, I stood in silence, sipping the beer and thinking about Becka and her problem with letting me get too close—letting anyone get too close. Yet, she was keeping me just close enough to want more.

I shook my head. I would never understand women.

I finished my beer and tossed the bottle in the contractor-sized recycling bin outside, which was overflowing with empty bottles. My eyes were ready to shut.

It was eleven fifteen at night.

Where the hell is Nick? I thought.

Whatever. Maybe the guy was getting laid. Good for him.

I brushed my teeth, excited that my pillow would still smell of Becka's dark hair. Like vanilla.

Chapter 7

The next morning, Nick's work truck was parked in the driveway, so he must have come home at some point during the night. His bedroom door was closed as I walked from the shower back to my room, and it remained closed as I headed out to the office.

The only change I made to the interior of that small space was to clear away some of the clutter: the rocks, crystals, and unopened junk mail that took up every inch of usable surface. The ledgers were stacked before me on the desk, and I got down to business.

I heated up a cup of tea while I went over the numbers. It was strange, I thought, that I loathed working in a cubicle, but now, in a not-so-different environment, I was really enjoying it. There was something about putting numbers in order, in a logical and controlled order, that was pleasing. Perhaps it was because the room didn't resemble a traditional office, or because I didn't have any coworkers walking around with painted smiles on their faces, lit up by those awful fluorescent lights that cast everyone with a cold blue hue.

I had begun doing the payroll when Becka's strange mood shift from the night before played over in my thoughts. Why the girl thought she was below anyone's standards was beyond me. She'd told me about a few of her past boyfriends, but mostly about this one guy named Jake whom she'd dated when she was only twenty. He was a surfer, who was apparently quite good, and had won some big competition in Hawaii when he was still in high school. Jake went out surfing one day and never came back. He got caught up in a wave and was knocked senseless by his board. They found his body miles down the shore, swept off by the riptide. There's no question that Jake's death had impacted Becka's life in a god-awful way, but the scope of that event was beyond me. She had dated several guys after Jake, but they'd all ended in typical mid-twenties disaster.

I took a sip of my now-lukewarm tea and thought that I would have to call Becka later on. Cheer her up. Maybe take her out for a beer.

My thoughts were distant as I studied the names on payroll, going down the list of employees. Something caught my attention—something was off. I read them over again, focusing, tapping each name with my pen to make them stick in my memory. Nick had everyone's time cards in a neat pile, as well as the list of percentages that changed regularly, as did the yield of the crop.

I read them over once more. Carpenter X was missing. Maybe Nick had just forgotten? Maybe …

Fragments of Nick's drunken debauchery from several weeks ago flashed in my memory: *"I'll get you! I'll g-get you! You're the last one, and I'll fucking* kill *you!"*

I shook the words out of my head.

It must be a mistake, I thought. Must be.

"… I'll fucking kill *you …"*

The bullet shots echoed in my mind, Nick wildly missing the bottle on the lawn until the chambers clanked empty.

No, no, no. No way. An accident. I was sure. I picked up my phone and dialed our house line. It rang once, and then I hung up.

Maybe I should just include his partner, and let it be remedied later. Or maybe I should write out the numbers exactly how Nick had written them.

I picked up my phone and dialed the house again. It rang and rang, and then a pleasant-sounding female robot said, *"Please leave a message for—"*

I hung up.

It was only right to include Carpenter X, right? I mean the guy was still showing up at our house every week like always …

… Had he been there this week? I tried to recall, but shit—I didn't remember seeing him parked out in the driveway. If that were true, and Carpenter X had not shown up, it would be the first time since I'd been living with Nick that the guy ever missed a week.

The office suddenly felt cold and entirely too small. The air smelled stagnant, like it had been trapped in that room forever. The dust motes were idling still in the shaft of light pouring down from the skylight.

I secured the ledger behind the cabinet, stepped outside, and locked the door behind me. A moment later I was driving fast toward home.

Chapter 8

The car engine was off, but I sat in the driveway for a while looking at Nick's truck parked next to mine. It hadn't moved since I'd left.

I got out of the car and walked to the house.

Inside, I could see straight across the house to the kitchen and to the back door, wide open. I crossed the room and stood in the doorway.

"Good morning," I said to Nick, who was sitting at the round picnic table smoking a cigarette.

He looked up, a smile cracking across his tired face.

"Hey, Powers, man."

"Rough night last night?" The red in his eyes glared even from this distance.

"Nah, nothing like that."

There was a gap of silence as he finished his cigarette, twisting it out on the ashtray. In that silence our thoughts were conveyed to each other more so than if we had spoken words out loud. He knew why I was standing there.

I spoke first. I said, "Hey, Nick—"

Then he interrupted. "I want you to come with me." He stood. "I have something to show you."

"Where?"

"Get changed."

I looked down at what I was wearing: a button-up shirt and pants. He walked past me toward his room wearing jean shorts and nothing else. I doubted the guy was even wearing underwear.

"What should I put on?"

"A suit," he shouted over his shoulder.

***

We took my car and Nick navigated.

"Take this left," he said, pointing.

For many miles I drove and he directed. He sat slumped in the passenger seat, wrinkling his suit jacket until I took a slight right on a quiet road and then another left, arriving at our destination. I swallowed, and my palms grew slippery on the wheel.

"This it?" I asked.

He nodded. "Right there, all those people."

Dozens of people stood gathered in a circle, all dressed in black. I parked at the end of a procession of cars, all pulled onto the grassy shoulder of the cemetery road. The lead car, the hearse, was nearly out of view.

Nick stared straight ahead as I looked over the mourning crowd. My mouth became dry.

I licked my lips, then asked, "This him?"

"Yup."

Nick didn't break his absent stare.

The grievers stood around an empty hole in the ground, ready to lower the casket to its final resting place. In the distance, I could discern a line of men standing straight-backed in matching uniforms, saluting.

"This guy serve?"

"No." Nick shook his head. "He's a cop. Was a cop."

My eyes went wide. "A *cop*? You were partnered with a *cop*?"

Nick nodded. "Didn't have a choice."

"And you ..." I didn't want to say the words. It was hard enough to fathom that my friend, my old hippie friend, was a killer ... but a *cop* killer?

"I didn't kill him," he muttered. "I know what you're thinking, but I swear on my life ... I didn't kill him."

I watched the people standing graveside as Nick elaborated. "He was a cop. Reached retirement last week. Died yesterday of a heart attack."

The coincidence of these events wasn't lost on me.

He continued, "Look, I know how this looks. I admit it, I wanted him dead, couldn't wait to see that fucker six feet under. But it wasn't me. I swear to Christ. He was worth more to the operation alive than dead."

"I don't get it. How does—"

"Listen, him being alive and in the force has kept our operation up and running. He was our security. He kept certain individuals away from our contacts and territories. All of our security guys were his men, employed by him."

I swallowed and said, "Hey, Nick, you gotta start telling me—what did this guy do to you? What's your deal with him?"

He was silent for a moment, his jaw clenching. Finally he spoke, "They busted me, back when I was young. Him and two other guys. They were crooked, even more so back then. He made me keep the operation up and running all these years. I didn't have a choice. I paid him—*them*—for protection. They kept the competition away and our business free from interference from the law. They did their jobs well, as you know. Our operation never hit a snag in all these years."

"Who are the other two?"

"They're dead. They're all dead. I'm the last one alive, and I would piss on their graves—I *have* pissed on their graves."

"So, you hate them because they busted you?"

Nick didn't answer.

"Look," I pleaded. "You got to start letting me know what's going on. You made me management for a reason, and I can't make logical decisions if you're keeping things from me."

Nick nodded, turning to watch the procession of mourners.

"All right," he said. "All right. You're right, so listen closely, I'm going to lay it all on you: that man rotting in his coffin, his name is Frank White. Since the mid-sixties he's been keeping a well-organized group of Russian businessmen away from the operation. For years now, Frank's told me that the Russians were no longer a threat, that their organization had dwindled down to the last few remaining men, and they were weak at best. Just a few low-level crooks. But now, with Frank's sudden death mere moments after his retirement, we gotta keep our eyes open."

I swallowed.

"You think the Russians are making a move?"

He shrugged. "Don't know. Back in the day, they moved fast. If they were going to plan a takeover, they would have already done more than kill the head of security. They would have made their presence known and their intentions recognized."

"So you don't think they killed Frank? Or do you?"

"Powers, man, I don't know."

"What's our move then?"

"We don't have one. Not yet. We don't know anything. For all we know, Frank drank too much at his retirement party and that old ticker of his finally gave out. It's not like that fat piece of shit took care of himself over the years. Shit like that happens, people just die sometimes. For now, we keep on working. Nothing changes."

I nodded.

Nick sighed. "I'm going to lay something else on you, something only two other people in the world know."

He turned and looked at me.

"All right ..."

"I'm, well." He sighed. "Frank White, he kept me in the operation. Jim too. That is to say, we haven't had a choice all of these years. That bastard, he's been pulling the strings since day one."

"You telling me you want out?"

"Powers." He glanced down at his feet. "I'm getting old. When I was eighteen, swinging dope on the streets, I never thought I'd wind up this deep in the business. I've ... wanted out for a long time now. Jim knows, and so does Darin, and now you do too. Darin was training to take charge, being groomed for ownership. This day was unavoidable, when Frank or myself would die and the operation would be leaderless."

"What did this guy have on you?"

Nick shook his head. "It doesn't matter now."

"All right, all right. So … what are you trying to say here? Is Darin coming back?"

"He'll be back sooner than later, I'm afraid to say. His mother isn't doing well last I spoke to him. When he returns, he'll take charge of the operation. The paperwork is already drafted. Until then, if anything happens to me, well, you're next in line. But only if you choose to accept the responsibilities."

I took a deep breath.

"What about Jim and Becka?"

"No," he said. "It's not a job for Becka. And Jim, he doesn't want the responsibility. He grows and I sell. That's the way we've always done business."

This was a lot to take in. Never had I thought about leading the operation. Hell, I'd only just been promoted to management, and I still didn't know jack shit about leadership. Learning the books and numbers, and growing the plants to Jim's meticulous specifications, would take time.

"Nick … of course I accept, but I don't think I'm ready."

"I know, I know. Look—I'm not leaving anytime soon. I'll teach you, starting tomorrow. When Darin comes back, he'll be put in charge and you'll be second in command. He'll take care of sales; you continue learning from Jim how to grow. Jim's not as young as he used to be, and despite his love for the job, for the plants, he'll be retiring one day too. It will be your job when that day comes. You and Darin will make a good team."

"And Becka, of course."

"Yes, yes. Of course. You're going to have to sign some paperwork at home, indicating that the deed to the property is to be transferred to you and Darin. It won't be binding until it's filed, or if something happens to me."

I nodded. "I understand."

"You have to keep this quiet. You understand?"

"Of course."

"Seriously. You don't mention anything to Becka. Nothing about Frank White, nothing about me retiring. I know you guys are close, but you have to keep your mouth shut. You can take that as your first lesson in management: keep your fucking mouth shut."

"I got it. I understand."

The only thought going through my mind was how badly I wanted to tell Becka everything. I wanted to call her right then and there and start babbling. Maybe some of the old office gossiping had rubbed off on me. But I knew Nick was right: leading a business such as ours requires a large degree of secrecy. I would do whatever needed to be done.

Then a thunderous cracking cut through the air. Nick and I flinched, looking over to the mass of people. The officers standing at attention had fired their rifles in unison. They fired twice more, and then stood rigid with their rifles out before them. I looked down at the suit I was wearing.

"Should we show our respects?"

Nick turned away from the funeral, sinking down in his seat. "Nah. Let's get out of here. Let the bastard rot."

Chapter 9

"I'm sorry about the way I acted."

Becka sounded tired over the phone. I could envision her just waking up after only a few hours of sleep from working the night shift, sipping a cup of coffee.

"Hey, don't be," I said between bites of my toast. "Look, I understand. I get down in the dumps sometimes too."

I wasn't particularly in the mood this morning to talk about our relationship, being that just yesterday Nick had laid a whole crazy heap of shit on my lap. But Becka needed someone to talk to, some reassurance that she didn't have a broken soul.

"When Sarah left me, I thought my life was over. Two years I gave that relationship. I know that isn't the longest time, but I had given it everything that I could. I thought she was the one."

"Yeah, I know. I think I'm just exhausted, Powers. I think you're exhausted too. We work a lot, and we work strange hours."

I nodded, even if she couldn't see me. "Working strange hours has been my life for a long time. Shit, I was working nights at the bar well before I moved in with Nick and Darin, before I took the office job."

"I remember."

She knew all of this, but I went on anyway just to take her mind somewhere else.

"Most nights I would get home at four, five if we were drinking—which we normally were. Hell, I remember some nights we'd be taking back shots as the sun was coming up, obliterated drunk. We'd see joggers and people walking their dogs still half-asleep out the windows, and then we'd all look at each other like, 'Shit, we gotta get out of here.' A few times, it was seven in the morning when we staggered out the door."

"Yeah, man, I remember those days. That's how we first met. What was the name of that band?"

"Dead Alive." She was referring to the cover band that used to play at Whiskey Sins, the bar I worked at. It was a relief when Dead Alive played; dealing with a bar full of stoners was way better than the usual assortment of bikers cranked out of their minds, wearing filthy leather jackets and vests all covered in patches that looked like they hadn't been removed for months. That bar was how I had first met Becka, Nick, and Darin. They came to every show, or at least Nick did, and Becka and Darin were there most of the time. Jim even showed up once in a while, lost in the sea of bearded vagabonds. I knew them as patrons before we became friends, and I started looking forward to seeing them at the bar. Half the time I was taking back shots with them. It was around that time when my girlfriend, Sarah, laid it all on me: she had fucked some guy named Tim, who I'd never even met. Anyway, I needed a place to stay, and Nick and Darin had a room.

"Yeah, that's it. Those guys played the Dead like you were right there listening to Jerry. That bar was great, man."

"Had a rough crowd. Whiskey Sins was the stomping ground of the Barren Souls."

"Oh Christ, those guys were bad news. They practically ran that place."

"No shit. They were snorting more coke and meth than they were selling. I never asked questions; I literally turned my back to not see. They tipped big for that, crisp hundreds on Budweisers. We got along good enough, for the most part. They listened to me when I had to cut one of them off. Well, most of the time. The owner, Barry, I'm sure they tipped him a lot more than they tipped me. We were told—all of the bar staff—to let the Barren Souls do as they please, sell whatever they were selling. Just no fights, no cops."

"I get the chills just thinking about them. Who was the leader of those guys again?"

"The president? Dale. Dale Erickson. Funny, the guy was the skinniest out of the bunch. But Jesus, man, you didn't want to fuck with him. I remember this one time, when a member of their gang made a joke about the stubble on Dale's face always being the same length, just a bit shaggy. Like he was purposely leaving it that way, concerned about his looks. When the guy pointed at Dale's face, laughing, thinking the joke was innocent, Dale fucking snapped his finger back in one quick motion. I was right there, saw his fingernail bend to touch his wrist in a fraction of a second."

"That's disgusting. I've heard some crazy shit about them over the years—armed robbery, arson, even kidnapping. Those guys didn't fuck around."

"I wouldn't doubt it. And Whiskey Sins was their bar. I stopped more fights and kicked more people out of that place than you could imagine—even the hippies. Must have been something in the water."

"Or the whiskey. Yeah, there were some heavy brawls there. It got you the job with Nick though. I remember him seeing you stop a confrontation between two big dudes before any punches were thrown. He was impressed. Said it took intelligence to stop a conflict before it turned violent."

"Maybe. He also knew I did some of the bookkeeping for the bar, so he knew I was good at math. Even before this recent promotion of sorts, Nick would ask me basic questions about spreadsheets and Quicken. Although, now I know that he never took his bookkeeping out of the pencil and paper era. I miss working at that bar sometimes, the hustle and bustle. Tending bar is the hardest job I ever had. The multitasking is insane, but I still have a love for it. When my adrenaline got pumping and the coffee or Red Bull kicked in, a certain euphoria would overtake me as I ran back and forth behind the line, pouring multiple drinks at a time, dealing with three, four orders at any given moment."

"Those were the days." She was sounding more positive. "Hey, you want to take a vacation, get away for a while? Just you and me. We could use it."

"A vacation? When are you thinking?"

"Today, man. Let's just get in the car and drive."

I finished my coffee and stood from the table, putting my plate in the sink. "Today? You want to get in the car and drive away somewhere?"

"Doesn't it sound like fun?"

"We have work, Becka."

"Nick would be cool with us taking a few days off. They could do without us for a little while, there aren't any big deliveries this week."

I swallowed. Damn, I wanted to tell her everything that Nick had told me yesterday. The words were fighting to get past my teeth.

"We really can't, Becka." I looked at the time glowing on the oven clock. "Shit, I gotta get going."

"Just think it over, Powers. We could get out of here, disappear for a while. Spend some time together."

Was I really hearing this? Was Becka being … romantic? Was she trying to get closer to me, when only a day ago she was in tears telling me I should move on, find someone to settle down with? Jesus, I did not—and will never—understand women. Not in the slightest.

"It sounds awesome, really. But I can't right now, Nick's expecting me at the warehouse. He left early this morning, I didn't even see him get up."

She sighed. "All right, man. All right."

"I'll call you later. We'll talk. What time you in?"

"Eight." The happiness I roused from her was disappearing.

"Look, maybe you do need a vacation. I'll mention it to Nick. We'll figure it out."

"Okay, man. Okay."

I looked at the time.

"I really got to go."

"I know."

We said goodbye, and I hightailed it to the door.

The coffee was kicking in as I drove through the woods. The sunshine was clear and bright. The air was crisp with the morning, yet warming up fast. I pushed down on the pedal, speeding through the familiar twisting roads until I approached the industrial section and saw the warehouse in the distance. The painted-over graffiti on the large sheet metal wall became more alive as I neared until I pulled around to the front of the building.

Nick's construction van was parked by the door, and I parked beside it, whistling the melody from the old *Looney Tunes* cartoons as I got out. Jim wasn't there yet; his white sedan was nowhere to be seen. A shiny black Cadillac was parked on the other side of Nick's van, and I eyed it up. Mark must have traded in his Benz. But then I started thinking. *Frank White dies, and then his security guy goes and buys a new car?* There was probably nothing to it. He had mentioned trading in the Benz, but still, I would mention it to Nick. We were on the lookout for anything suspicious, after all.

Typing my code in the lock, I looked over my shoulder again at the Cadillac and stepped inside the building.

I was about to ask Mark, "New car?" but as I turned around I heard the sudden scraping of the folding chair against the cement ground.

"What—?" was all I got out as a wide, built man whom I had never seen before stood up before me, his eyes wide as he pulled an automatic pistol from his holster and aimed it squarely at my head.

"Jesus Christ," I muttered, my hands reaching up involuntarily.

"Stop! Stop right there. Don't move!" His thick Russian accent echoed down the hallway.

The door slammed shut behind me, cutting off the vibrant sun and the warm springtime air.

Chapter 10

The Russian looked angry, and yet calm. Like waving a gun in a person's face was an everyday event.

"Don't fucking move!" he screamed.

"My name is Evan Powers. *Evan Powers!* I work here!" I stared in disbelief at the pistol barrel aimed before my eyes. "Where's Nick?"

"Shut your fucking mouth!"

I did as instructed.

The sudden clopping of footsteps came rushing from down the hallway, and a second large man, taller than the first, ran in from around the corner of the packaging and distribution room. He was carrying a pistol, and as he approached, he asked the other man in a Russian accent, "Who is he?"

"Who are you?" the man pointing a gun commanded.

"Evan. Evan Powers."

The taller Russian pulled a piece of paper from his pocket and studied it.

"He's management," he said. "Turn around. Hands on the wall."

My palms were slippery against the cold sheet-metal wall.

"What's going on here?" I said, trying not to let my shaking voice show.

"Shut your mouth."

Hands patted me down, went into my pockets. My wallet was taken.

"Turn around, sit in the chair."

I sat in the folding chair and looked at the men. They were beasts in black leather jackets, clean-cut, with stony-looking faces. Mafia, I presumed.

The thing about fear is that it can turn quickly to anger, especially when you're backed up against a wall. But at the moment, I knew I had to suppress whatever violent urges passed through my mind. I saw flashes of myself quickly standing up, twisting the pistol out of the man's hand, and liberating the warehouse … but I knew in reality I would be killed immediately.

The taller man went back down the hall, the way he had come, saying something in Russian to the other man over his shoulder. When he was out of earshot, I asked the man standing before me, "What's your name?"

The man just looked at me.

"I told you mine, what's yours?"

The man smirked.

"Where's Nick?"

He shrugged.

"Not the chatty type, huh?"

"Why don't I put a bullet in your mouth, see how chatty you are then. Hmm?"

I looked around the entry hallway.

"Where's Mark?"

"Remember what I said about the bullet in your mouth? Try me."

I looked at him, and decided it was in my best interest to be the strong silent type.

A moment passed and I turned at the sound of footfalls. The tall Russian approached.

"You can wait for Mr. Grady outside."

"Why don't you tell me what's going on here?"

"You can talk to Nick when he's ready."

I swallowed but didn't stand. I wanted some answers. I demanded some explanation—

In a swift motion, the large Russian pushed my chair forward, making me stand. He opened the door, and the shorter Russian walked toward me.

It only took two steps until I was outside.

"Your entry code is being erased as we speak," the tall man said, and then shut the door.

Outside, the warm air felt hot.

"Jesus Christ," I said out loud, staring at the door, feeling like it would open back up again at any moment. But it didn't. Minutes passed like they were made of molasses, and I walked back and forth between my car and the door, checking my watch every thirty seconds and glancing up at the security camera mounted above the entrance.

As promised, my security code blinked red—denied—when I tried typing it in. Nick had given me the master code, and my finger hesitated over the dial, but I relented. If the master code had not been erased, I wasn't going to simply give it to these guys.

The longer I waited, the deeper my mind went to dark places. I thought about guns and knives, and whether or not I should try to get a few and kick the door down. But again, the reality of the situation was that I would be shot dead no more than two steps in.

There was a pay phone about a block away near the UPS warehouse, and I contemplated driving over there to call Jim or Becka, or somebody. Fuck, I wished I had Mark's number. And where the hell was he anyway? Where was security? Had the Russians killed him? Was there any blood around the entrance, any signs of a struggle? I had to start noticing these things; I had to start acting like management—

The door swung open. It happened so fast that for a brief moment I froze, and then out walked Nick. The guy was as white as a sheet of paper.

"Nick—Nick!" I ran over to him. "Nick, what's going on, what's—"

"Powers, come with me. Keep your voice down."

I looked around. "There's nobody here. Nobody can hear me."

"Get in the van." Nick walked over to the driver's side door and got in, reaching across the cab to unlock the passenger's side.

I was in the van in a flash.

"Nick ..."

"They made a move. The Russians killed Frank, poisoned him. They got every bit of information out of him that they could. They killed the one man left who could keep them at bay."

"Oh, Jesus Christ. What do we do? We can't fight them—are we supposed to fight them? Nick, I'm not sure—"

"No," he hissed, "we are *not* going to fight them."

"How did they get the information from Frank? Did they torture him? What information do they have?"

"I don't know. Not completely. But they have a lot. They know everything that Frank knew: our names, addresses, pay, our profits." He stopped to swallow and then pulled a pack of cigarettes from his breast pocket, dragging one out from the pack with his teeth and offering me the pack. I took it greedily.

"I guess you could say they tortured him, in a sense. They used some drug called devil's breath. I never heard of it until today."

I racked my memory, but I had never heard of it either.

"What is it?"

"It's a tree of some sort. They told me it has beautiful white flowers, but that doesn't matter." He took a long inhale, flicking the ashes out the window. "The stuff is turned into a white powder which can be put in food, drinks, or as is the case with Frank, it was simply blown in his face. It takes mere moments—a minute or two—until the effects kick in." He ground his cigarette out in the ashtray and pulled another from the pack. "The stuff is crazy. They call it the zombie drug in Columbia. Turns you mindless and your memory's erased. You'll do whatever the person asks of you while you're all fucked up."

"What do you mean?"

"I mean, they literally turned Frank into a zombie. He willingly gave them all the information he had on the operation."

"No way."

"I'm serious. They showed me a video. Just a clip they took during his interrogation. All they did was ask Frank for information and he gave it, like they were just chatting. They sat down at a table, Frank with his hands crossed, and they talked leisurely."

"How have I never heard of this shit?"

"Because, Powers," he said, looking at me, "it's extremely fucking rare. They said they got it from some KGB guy. Criminals use it to empty people's bank accounts, with the person simply walking up to an ATM and handing over the money. It's also used as a date-rape drug, and the person won't remember a thing."

"My God."

He nodded. "Then they told Frank to take his insulin. I never knew he was diabetic, but it's no surprise—the guy was a fat piece of shit. Then they told him to take it again."

"He had a heart attack from taking insulin?"

"Not directly. They said they were going to make him shoot himself if necessary, make it look like a suicide, but they wanted to try something new. They said they wanted to try something … fun, exciting. The insulin made him tremble, vomit … he had a seizure. They showed me." He took another long drag. "They'll never find the drug, the devil's breath, in the toxicology report. There's no reason to even look for it."

"So, what do we do?"

"It's game over, man, it's end times. Listen … I told them that I was glad Frank White was dead, whether of natural causes or not—I don't care. If Frank is no longer around to keep me working, well, fuck it. Without Frank they have us outnumbered."

"How many are there?"

"Not sure. Just now, I met with two bosses, and the big guys in the hallway are both lieutenants. I saw a few people go into the grow room, probably botanists. And a few low-level security guys. Kids, really. But I have no idea of their total numbers."

"Just yesterday you told me all this shit about Darin taking over, about me stepping up."

"Did you not hear what I just told you? What they did to Frank? These are dangerous people, Powers. The Russians are taking over the business— they already have taken over—and they're letting me retire. And not just myself, but everyone: you, Jim, Becka."

My mind was in a whirl, and I was starting to feel dizzy.

"Give me another cigarette." I reached my hand out, and he gave me the pack.

"They have some conditions," Nick went on. "We have to sell off our remaining product, transfer all distribution channels, and hand over the keys. They are businessmen, after all. They are going to give us a percentage of our final stock as a payoff and then send us on our way."

"They're going to pay us? I just … don't know what to think. I can't believe this is happening."

"Powers, man." Nick sighed. "Business takeovers happen, either by legal means or not. Shit, just think of all the big corporations out there, using deceit, betrayal, or legal loopholes to send each other off to jail just to make more money for themselves. Not to mention we're damn lucky they stopped the killing at Frank. It's rare to see a takeover go down with this little bloodshed. I know it's hard for you to see the big picture, but this is the best course of action. Really, it is. I've … I've been wanting out for years. I couldn't get out, wasn't allowed to get out. These guys, these Russians, we don't want to try and merge with them, become partners. They aren't people we want to get involved with. They might be weaker now than they were in the sixties, but they're still very dangerous. With Frank around, I haven't been keeping tabs on them over the years. I have no idea of their reach. We can't fight them. I'm so sorry to get you involved. You quit your office job, I made you promises … and now all this shit happens. But look—you'll get a healthy share of profits from this last delivery, enough to see you off safely. You'll be fine. You'll land on your feet. You'll survive to work another day." He paused. "You have no idea how important that last statement is. If we fight these guys we'll all wind up dead. You, me … even Becka. You're young. You have a future ahead of you."

"Okay," I said. "Okay." I tried to calm my conflicting thoughts. My dad would have belted my ass for turning my back on a fight, but this was different. This wasn't a fistfight—this was a war involving silenced pistols and shadows. As far as being out of work, well, Nick was right: surviving to find another job was better than winding up dead. And if Becka could possibly get hurt in all this, it wasn't worth the risk. A flash of thought went through my mind: the drug, the devil's breath, Becka … rape. Anger boiled inside me along with a deep sadness.

"Hey," I said. "Maybe it's for the best."

Nick cracked a wayward smile. "Glad you see the big picture. There's only one last thing … delivering the final stock. Deliveries are made as a two-man team. Powers, man …" He didn't want to say it. "They demanded that Jim and I go, as usual, but when I called Jim, well, he hung up on me after hearing about the Russians. Jim was around back when these guys had more power—he remembers them well. He's gone. Jim's gone, man. Everyone else is gone too, the entire operation. Our security personnel were all Frank's guys. With their boss dead, nobody showed up for work today. All the Russians had to do was hack the security keypad and walk in."

"So, you want me to go with you on the delivery?"

"No. Powers." He looked into my eyes. "You coming is the *last* thing that I want. But then you went and showed up at the warehouse just at the right moment. The Russians are demanding that you go. I tried calling you at home, but you must have left already. I called Becka, too."

"What did she say?"

"She didn't pick up. Sleeping, I presume. She worked last night. I left her a message, told her to take a few days off, that we hit a snag. Nothing big. I didn't want to explain anything over the machine."

I thought about my conversation with Becka earlier that morning.

"I don't think she'll have a problem taking a few days off. It will do her some good. Being out of work, though … I don't know how she'll handle that."

"We can worry about that later. I'll call her from the road, tell her the lowdown."

I nodded, thinking that I would call Becka the first chance I got.

Nick went on. "I'm going to make the delivery alone. I'll be fine. Fuck them."

I took a breath then said, "Like hell you are. It's a two-man job. I'm going with you, and we'll make the delivery together. End of story."

Nick shook his head. "Powers …"

"End of discussion."

He rubbed the bridge of his nose. "All right, man. All right. You and me."

"Where is the delivery going anyway?"

"British Columbia."

"Wait—*Canada?* How are we going to cross the border?"

"Same way I always cross it. We'll meet Darin in Montana and make the trip over the border on foot. I've done it plenty of times; we're dropping off to an established contact. Darin came up with the route when he was a kid and used to sneak over the border with his friends. I called him just now, told him what went down. He's expecting me—expecting us."

I let out a sigh.

Processing these events would take some time. My life had just been flipped upside down and I was hovering somewhere in midair. I couldn't desert Nick; he was a friend—a good friend. Many of our degenerate friends considered Nick a father figure since the guy could offer guidance and advice to all the young screwups. But I didn't see him that way.

One night, a while back, I told him, "No, man, I had a dad already. I don't see you as a father."

"All right," he said.

"You're my brother, man. You're my brother … my best friend."

Nick had looked taken aback, but then he leaned in and whispered, "Thank you, Powers. My God, thank you. I can't be a father to any more of you screwups."

So I felt confident in my decision, knowing full well that it involved a large degree of risk. But if it would get us all out of trouble, especially Becka, I would do whatever was necessary.

I asked Nick, "When do we leave?"

"Tonight," he said. "We leave tonight."

Chapter 11

The first thing I did when I got home was call Becka. When the answering machine began talking to me, I hung up. This wasn't the sort of message to leave as a voice mail. I checked our own answering machine, but there was nothing from her.

We were leaving immediately, so I grabbed my duffel bag from the top shelf of the hallway closet, smacked away a layer of dust, and began stuffing a few items of clothing inside. The only toiletries I packed were my toothbrush, deodorant, and a comb. A razor wouldn't be needed. I would either buy a disposable on the road or not bother shaving at all.

Nick was outside waiting for me, and when he saw me approach he started up the engine. I tossed my duffel bag behind the passenger seat and climbed in.

"You ready?" he asked.

"Hell no."

With that, he put the truck in drive and crept along the driveway until we were out on the main road.

"You call Becka?" I asked.

"I tried, but she didn't pick up. I left another message."

"What'd you say?"

"I was vague. I told her that you and I were taking a road trip, and would be back in a few days."

He knew that I had tried to call her as well, but he didn't ask if we spoke. He knew that we hadn't. Sooner or later I was going to have to get a cell phone, but the things looked annoying, clunky. I hated the feeling of my keys in my pocket; I couldn't imagine something as cumbersome as a telephone rubbing against my leg all day.

"You think she's gone somewhere? She was talking about needing a vacation this morning."

Nick shrugged.

"She said I need a vacation too." I let out a laugh.

"Is that right?" He laughed too, in something of a huff. "This is a hell of a vacation you're going on."

"You're not kidding."

Out on the highway, Nick sped to the industrial section and pulled into the warehouse parking lot. He passed the main entrance, where the same black Cadillac sat parked along with two other cars that I didn't recognize, and drove further toward the rear of the building. We pulled up next to a set of sliding garage doors.

Nick got out of the truck and I followed.

He typed his code in the security keypad and the cargo doors swung open. Directly across the hall was the break-room door. Inside, there was another door on the left leading to packaging and shipping. This room I was familiar with, having spent countless nights weighing and packaging herb with Becka … as well as doing some very dirty things on that break-room table. That same table where now the tall Russian from earlier sat sipping a cup of coffee. I recognized the chipped handle of the mug as a cup I'd often used. A flush of anger rose in my chest, but I suppressed it away.

"Mr. Grady and Mr. Powers," the tall guy said. "Right on time." He smiled and stood, leaving the mug on the table, the vapors trailing in the air. I tried not to look at it.

"Yeah," Nick said. "Let's get on with it."

We walked in, and I stepped cautiously through the doorway.

Nick propped the break-room door open with a stopper and did the same to the second door.

The tall Russian gave Nick a clipboard with the weight and amount of product. Nick only glanced at it before dropping it on the table.

The tall man shrugged. "Just be sure all of it arrives at the destination. Now hurry up, you need to get moving. We'll be talking real soon." The man walked to a door in the rear of the warehouse leading to the office and where all of the security monitors were set up on a desk, and he disappeared, closing the door behind him. I could hear voices speaking in Russian through the wall.

"Come on," Nick said. "Let's move."

We walked into the packaging room to look at our haul. A long wooden table took up much of the room's interior, with strips of rope going from one side to the other along the far wall. This was where the plants were hung to dry, the leaves trimmed, and the herb cut to manageable pieces. The drying process took two weeks or so, but it was never rushed. Drying was just as important as any of the other steps in the plant's life cycle. When the branches were a bit crisp and could snap, no longer moist and flexible, they were ready to be further trimmed down on the table. On the wall beside the entrance were shelves for Becka's glass jars.

The thick aroma of marijuana was as pungent as ever, but all the plants had been removed from the drying line—no matter their stage—cut down, vacuum sealed, and stuffed into cardboard boxes. Some of Becka's jars were empty, but not all of them. I could practically feel her shock and anger, as if she were seeing this barbaric intrusion herself. Her hours of careful study over each and every bud, meticulously taking notes on each jar's progression, only to have them befouled by the filthy hands of these lowlifes.

"She'd have a heart attack," I said, pointing to an empty jar.

Nick only glanced, shaking his head. "Can't think of that now."

He picked up a box and began carrying it through the break room and outside to the van. I wasn't sure how many trips we made, but when we finished the rear of the truck was packed—and I mean crammed full—with boxes of vacuum-sealed bags of herb stacked like brickwork.

We closed the door to the warehouse and left through the break room. I peered around the corner, looking down the hallway toward the main entrance before stepping outside. "No one's watching the door."

"Who cares, Powers?" He nodded to one of the security cameras. "Let's get out of here."

Nick put the van in drive and swung back toward the highway. I looked over my shoulder as we passed the warehouse.

"This is it, huh?"

"Yeah," he replied in a whisper. "This is it. Take a good look."

It was hard not to feel nostalgic—not to mention angry that my work at the operation would be over after this delivery and my newfound position as manager would be null and void.

But that's life, I suppose. People get fired all the time, and they go on with their lives.

"Getting dark soon," I said, looking at the sky as we merged onto the interstate. "We have about an hour before nightfall."

Nick craned his eyes at the dark blue sky.

"We won't get far tonight," he said. "Maybe across Pennsylvania, but not much farther."

"I don't mind driving through the night," I offered. "If we stop for coffee, I can put in some distance."

"The night is exactly when I *don't* want us driving. A single car driving along the interstate stands out. It's better to drive during the day, get lost in the herd."

The dark sky soon faded to absolute black as we put miles behind us. Nick chain-smoked cigarettes and I lit up a cigar, letting the time pass along with the shadowy scenery blazing by the windows. Conversation was minimal.

When it was near ten thirty, Nick turned down the radio.

"All right," he said. "Next town with a hotel, we're stopping."

"Sounds good."

Tunnel vision from the dark road soaring under the wheels of the car, along with the bright reflectors dotting the interstate in perfectly spaced intervals, had sent my mind into a hypnotized wander. A few cold beers followed by a long and uninterrupted sleep sounded unimaginably good. My mind was frazzled by the day's events. I couldn't imagine what Nick was thinking.

A blue highway sign whizzed by, indicating that the next town over had two hotels, four gas stations, and a host of fast-food restaurants.

We stayed that first night in a crummy room that smelled like mildew. We each tried calling Becka from a pay phone by the office, but we again only got her answering machine.

Nick parked the van as close to our room as possible and took the bed nearest the window so he could constantly peek out through the parted blinds.

We heated cans of soup for dinner using a small collapsible camping stove and ate on our separate beds while sipping beers. When Nick finished, he put his bowl on the nightstand and went to the window to stare down at the van, half-illuminated under a streetlight.

"Nothing's going to happen," I told him, flipping through the channels.

Nick nodded. "I know," he said, and came back to his bed, popping open a fresh beer.

"Here." I tossed the remote onto his mattress. "Get some sleep. The van has an alarm, so stop worrying."

"Yeah, I know." He took a long swallow from the bottle. "You go ahead and shut your eyes, I'll be doing the same shortly."

***

When I woke up Nick was still under his blankets, but when he heard me moving around, he jolted out of bed.

"You sleep?" I asked, yawning.

"Enough. Why don't you shower? I'll put coffee on. Let's get out of here."

I showered and brushed my teeth, and came back into our little room to see Nick already gone. I dressed and poured the remainder of the coffee he'd made into a Styrofoam cup, securing it with a traveling lid. Grabbing my duffel bag, I looked around the room for anything left behind.

I sipped the coffee by the door and nearly spit it back out.

"What is this shit?" I said aloud, leaving the cup on the dresser before shutting the door.

Outside, Nick was standing against the idling van, smoking a cigarette and rolling up the sleeves of his denim shirt.

"We're stopping for coffee," I shouted from the railing.

"I made coffee."

I shook my head. "That shit ain't coffee."

Nick rolled his eyes. "All right, let's get moving."

***

We drove straight through Chicago, not stopping. Nick got edgier, jumpier, the closer we got to cities and towns. I felt the same. The traffic, even miles away from Chicago, grew thick like mud, causing our paranoia to spike like crests on a wave, and wash over our bodies. We were having flashes of the what-ifs. *What if* we get into an accident? *What if* we get pulled over? *What if* that blue sedan over there veers into our lane, causing us to smack against the guardrail? How would we explain the copious amount of illegal drugs tucked away in the back of the truck? The answer was that we wouldn't. We would stick out our wrists and let the cold metal bind us.

I tried not to think of such things as the traffic swarmed around us, but a sheen of cold sweat covered my skin nonetheless.

As we passed the heart of Chicago from the interstate, it felt as if we'd just made the slow ascent to the top of a roller coaster, and were now soaring back down to the earth.

I turned to Nick. "Got a cigarette?"

His eyes were large, and he was staring out the windshield, his knuckles white from gripping the steering wheel.

"Help yourself."

I took a cigarette and lit it up, cracking the window. Nick did the same, but his movements were erratic.

"I'll drive next shift," I said, and pointed to the gas gauge. "We need a fill-up anyway."

Nick nodded. "Yeah, brother."

He pulled over at the next exit and went into the convenience store while I filled the tank. When he came back his eyes were puffy and red, and he looked gaunt, disheveled.

"You sleep at all last night?"

"Enough."

"Not enough."

I took the keys and started the engine. Only a mile back on the interstate, Nick fell into a fitful sleep. He jarred awake often, his eyes darting around the van's interior like a caged bird before drifting back to troubled dreams.

I turned the radio up, letting the music drown away his thoughts.

The miles flew by under the speeding tires along with the hours in the day. At some stage, close to Madison, Wisconsin, a deep snore issued from his throat, and continued on until the evening approached.

When he awoke, he looked out the window as if still in the deep pits of slumber.

"How long was I out?" he rasped, clearing his throat.

By the look on his face he wasn't sure if the dark blue sky indicated the coming of night or the beginning of morning.

"I don't know," I said. "Six hours, maybe seven?"

We pulled over to fill up the tank and Nick took the wheel. We found a campground to sleep for the night as the sky became dark. Once the fire got going in the fire pit and we gathered enough wood to last a few hours, we unrolled our sleeping bags and heated our dinner before the flames.

The sky was limitless and the stars too plentiful to grasp. Staring upwards, a calm feeling finally settled in my body, like I could somehow escape these recent stresses of life, and drift up and out of this world, to meld with the vastness of the universe.

Sleep that night was long and deep.

Chapter 12

We finally got a hold of Becka just outside of Madison, Wisconsin. The large college town was booming with bars and beers, but we stayed clear of temptation and drove further on across the rolling green hills outside of the city.

I sat in the passenger seat of the van, parked across the expansive lot of a gas station, and watched Nick hold the receiver of a pay phone to his ear. Suddenly his posture changed and I could see his mouth moving. My heart began to race. I would have to wait to speak to her until he was done, give them some privacy—he was still her boss, after all. My hand gripped the handle of the door.

It was hard to discern his facial expressions, and after a minute he turned his back to me, resting his shoulder against the side of the telephone booth.

"Come on, Nick. Hurry up."

A few more minutes passed, and Nick dug into his pocket to feed the pay phone some change. Then he turned and waved me over.

I was out of the van in a flash, reaching out for the receiver.

Nick held his palm over the microphone and whispered, "She's pissed."

I took the phone and waited for him to cross the lot, lighting a cigarette.

"Becka?"

"Powers—*what the fuck!*"

I gulped. "Hey, Becka, I'm just as upset as you—"

"What the fuck are you doing making a delivery? Where are you—in fucking Wisconsin?"

"Look, I didn't have a choice. Did Nick explain everything to you?"

"He explained enough." My ears burned with her anger. "So, we're done—through. We're out of work. Is that it?"

"Well, we're—"

"Because *he* wants to throw in the towel?"

"It's not like that … not exactly. These people, these Russians, we don't want to fuck with them. These aren't people we should partner with."

"How do you know? Did you actually talk to them? Or are you just going by what Nick's telling you?"

"Well, I had one of them wave a gun in my face."

A robotic operator cut through our conversation.

"Please insert thirty-five cents for an additional four minutes."

"Hold on," I said before rummaging through my pockets and inserting some change.

The line cleared.

"They waved a gun at you?"

"Hey, Becka—have *you* talked to them? What's to make you think these guys are anything but ruthless?"

"No, I haven't talked to them." She sighed. "I don't know. Jesus man, I'm sorry. You shouldn't be out there making this delivery. It's sketchy. What are you thinking? You don't make deliveries. That's Nick and Jim's job."

"Jim skipped town."

"I'm worried." Her tone was becoming subdued. "You up and vanished, and I didn't know where you went."

"I tried to call you, several times. We both did. Where have you been?"

"I got Nick's message about taking some time off, so that's exactly what I did. I went to Atlantic City for a few days, blew off some steam. I thought you had talked to him, and the whole thing about hitting a snag at the operation was just some bullshit Nick was making up since he was leaving a message. I called you before I left, both at home and at the warehouse. I wanted you to come, but you didn't pick up, and you were real adamant about not being able to get away. So I left. When I got home, I heard Nick's message about you guys on a road trip and a bunch of missed calls from strange numbers."

"They were pay phones."

"I figured that much. I went to your house, and even to the warehouse."

"Stay away from there. Seriously, Becka."

"Well, no-fucking-shit, Powers. My security code wouldn't work, and there were a bunch of dark luxury cars parked outside. Gave me the chills, man."

"Everyone's gone, Becka. It's over. It's all over."

"Yeah, I got that." Her anger was back, but then she relented. "Powers, you shouldn't be making this delivery."

This conversation wasn't going anywhere. I sighed audibly enough for her to hear, and said, "I know. I know. I got it."

There was silence following. She was upset, but none of this was my fault. Never before had she been this protective over me … or was she jealous that I was out there and not her? She wasn't the type of girl who liked to sit on the sidelines, watch the action pass her by.

"Look," she said, "so why are you on this delivery? Has anyone talked to Jim?"

"I don't know, Becka. Nick talked to him, and like I said, he split town. There's no one left. It's a two-man job, and the Russians demanded that I go. I have to be here."

"They demanded it? Look, just be careful, okay? Get home soon. I don't like this."

"I don't like this any more than you do, but hey—the sooner we make the drop-off, the sooner we can get on with our lives."

"What lives?"

I rolled my eyes. "Things will work out, Becka. Trust me. We'll find work. We're young, and we're lucky the Russians are letting us off the hook. We're even getting a percentage of this last sale. Nick went over the numbers with me; they're more than fair. We'll all have enough money to make ends meet until we find jobs."

"Maybe."

I looked over my shoulder to Nick, who was grinding out his finished cigarette in the dirt.

"Hey," I said. "I gotta get going."

"Yeah, okay. Please be careful."

"I'll be fine. I *am* fine. I'll call you first chance I get."

I hung up and took a deep breath. Nick waited for me by the van, his eyebrow raised inquisitively.

"Yeah," I said. "She's pissed."

"Sure as shit," he replied, and walked around to the driver's side.

Chapter 13

Nick seemed more himself the farther on we drove. He sang along with the music and tapped the steering wheel in rhythm. I read from a book I'd picked up at a gas station and smoked cigars and cigarettes for hours on end. Despite the ever-growing feeling of apprehension and anxiety that came along with carting tens of thousands of dollars' worth of drugs, the openness of the country and the sheer beauty of the vast plains of South Dakota going into the Black Hills of Wyoming had a way of settling my nerves.

We found camp before sunset outside of Devils Tower. The massive stone column of the breathtaking geological formation jutted out from the earth to dominate the landscape.

"Folklore says it was bears that made those marks on the rock." Nick pointed to the tower.

"Who said that?"

"Indians. Their story goes that these little girls were out playing when they see these bears coming at them, so they start to run. They climb up a rock and pray to their gods to save them, and sure as shit, their gods start growing the rock from under their feet. The bears scratched at the rock as it grew, trying to get at the girls, and that's what those deep gorges are along the tower. Bear claw marks."

The tower was directly before us, and I stared hypnotically at the columns of rock that gave Devils Tower its familiar striped appearance.

"Would have been some enormous bears," I said.

Nick laughed. "Sure as shit."

"How'd you know that?"

He shrugged. "Think Jim told me, not sure."

I nodded and smiled, thinking of Jim dancing around the garden of plants, holding the thick, murky soil in his hands as if it were a delicate flower. *Gold.*

Nick tossed a few splits of wood on the fire, and the dry wood took to the flames immediately.

As the night approached and the sky turned dark, we began to see faint pops of light on the far horizon, like sudden noiseless explosions so distant over the expansive terrain that they were barely recognizable. Slowly, the flashes grew brighter until we knew for certain that it was lightning we were seeing.

"Looks like we're sleeping in the van," I said, watching Nick crane his head at the coming light.

"Reckon so."

The lightning came out of the distant clouds like spiderwebs come alive, filling the sky with mazes of brilliant zigzags that were too expansive to fully witness. The black outline of Devils Tower at night stood out against the blinding strobes in shadowy wonder; the bolts issued forth from behind the mountain in a breathtaking spectacle of nature at its most awesome.

Rain never came, but a sharp wind swept over the ground, rustling the flames of the campfire into a fury of dazzling sparks.

"Ain't this some shit?" Nick said over the howling wind.

"Yeah."

The storm crept overhead, yet it never dropped more than a sprinkle of rain. Nick and I sipped from a flask-sized bottle of whiskey, passing the bourbon back and forth across the fire.

He stared off into the dizzying array of sparks, the lightning illuminating the campground in flashes.

"My partner," he said. "He was a cop. Crooked."

I took a sip from the bottle.

"I was swinging dope, just a kid. Eighteen years old. I didn't know any better. Pot was everywhere, and it only came natural to start selling the stuff. Me and my friends, we started small, a few bags at a time. The bags got larger, and our clientele list quickly grew. Before we knew it we were moving large quantities, ounces turned to pounds, and money started pouring in. Next we started a grow room, just small quantities to begin with. It didn't take long until the big swingers took notice of us; I mean the guys who were supplying the massive amounts of dope straight from Mexico. One of those groups was an up-and-coming Russian organization, led by two brothers in their early twenties. Me and my two partners—"

"Carpenter X?"

Nick shook his head. "No, no. Not Carpenter X. Not yet."

I nodded, realizing by the downward tone in his voice and his absent stare that if I were ever to hear Nick's story I would have to let him speak uninterrupted.

The lightning that seemed to emerge from Devils Tower flickered across the sky, booming thunder across the valley.

Nick continued. "We were all just kids. They were nineteen and twenty, and I was eighteen. I ran away from home when I was seventeen and got a room with them. The times then were … different, chaotic. My mother and father were all too happy to have their screwup son out of their house. The revolutionary counterculture did not sit well with them. My father was happy—actually happy—that the conflict in Vietnam was escalating. He believed that every generation had its war, a chance for the youth to sculpt themselves into men. He thought Vietnam would cure the curse of the times, convert the good-for-nothing hippies into clean-cut good-ole boys." Nick shook his head. "Anyway, my partners—friends—we set up shop in our apartment and rented a storage room to grow some crops. Jim Hoffman, he did all of our growing, even back then. We had an arrangement with Jim that he could stay in the grow room and not do any of the buying or selling. All he did was grow, and he was damn good at it."

A brilliant flash of lightning filled the sky, and Nick paused as the thunder crackled. A moment later, he continued. "It was a Tuesday afternoon, and we were all at the kitchen table, scaling out our product, when we hear a bang at the door—a loud bang, along with a crack. Someone kicked the door off its hinges, and before we had a chance to do anything other than flinch, four men stormed inside, guns drawn, shouting and screaming in Russian accents. They slammed our heads down on the table and pressed pistols to our temples."

Nick took a swig from the bottle and looked straight across the fire into my eyes.

"I've never been so terrified in all my life. They got us all kneeling on the ground in a neat row, hands on our heads, when in walk these two young Russian guys. Real slick types wearing tailored suits with neatly combed hair. They towered above us. The three of us were trembling on the ground, and I remember the feeling of my bladder about to explode. I kept telling myself, 'Don't piss yourself, Nick. Please, by God, don't piss yourself.' Some of the thugs went around our apartment, tossing all our weed and money into duffel bags while the others stood straight across from us, their pistols hovering before our faces. One of the bosses introduced himself as Vitali. The other one says his name is Nikolay. They were brothers, and they were in charge of this budding organization. Vitali starts talking, saying some things that we already knew and some other things that we did not know. We were on their turf, selling to their contacts. It was not a good situation for us. He told us he was taking our product and money. He told us he was going to have to bring us to the woods and shoot us in the backs of our heads. He told us he wasn't sure for how long we would have to be tortured before ending our lives. He mentioned things like razor blades under fingernails, hammers to balls, toes slowly pulled from the socket, broken elbows, fingers, and things involving pliers and blowtorches. One of their guys brings in this little red toolbox and opens the clasps, and Vitali starts displaying an assortment of tools. He holds up a screwdriver, inspecting the sharpness of the chipped head with his thumb, and my one partner starts pleading, crying and jabbering. The Russians laugh. They tell us it doesn't matter what we say or tell them— torture and death were already a sure thing, a contract set in stone. We should accept our demise and try to endure the pain until we fainted or bled out. Then, in a well-practiced motion, these guys had our hands behind our backs, gags in our mouths, and hoods over our heads. They grabbed me under my ribcage and pushed me across the room. I could hear birds outside, barely audible through the beating of my heart. They shoved us in the back of a van and took off. For a while I bounced and rolled around, unable to stop myself from falling over.

"We stopped somewhere quiet. No sounds of cars or people—nothing other than the rustling of trees. Hands grabbed me. I was forced out of the van and shoved to my knees. A gun pressed to where my spine and head met. My hood was ripped off and I looked up to see Vitali and Nikolay standing before the three of us, their hands clasped behind their backs as if they were leisurely glancing at a garden of flowers and not three kids, shaking and crying out for their mothers behind gags … pissing themselves. Then Vitali says, as if he were a judge and jury, 'You have been found guilty of infringing on our turf, and in doing so you have forfeited your lives.'

"The three of us started wailing, and after a brief pause, Nikolay quiets us, and says that maybe they'd had a change of heart. He says that they discussed the situation during the drive, and have decided to give us a choice: we could end things right then and there in the woods … or we could work for them. Sell *their* product and only *their* product. We would take orders directly from Nikolay and Vitali. We would never again venture out on our own, for they now owned our business, owned our lives. However, he went on to explain that if we stayed loyal we would be rewarded. Now, of course when they tore off our gags we all shouted and swore our allegiance. Who wouldn't? We didn't have a choice. It was all for show, the whole abduction, but we didn't know any better at the time. We were young. Way too young to be involved in such a business."

Nick paused to take another swig from the bottle, and passed the bourbon across the frenzied flames.

I didn't know what to say. Jesus Christ—these were the same guys we were now carting a boatload of drugs cross the US for. In essence, we were working for them.

"Nick," I said. "That's some crazy—"

A clap of thunder cut my words short. We both flinched at the noise. Raindrops began hitting the ground in grape-sized droplets, hissing and sizzling against the burning wood.

Nick stood. "Think it's time to go in the van. Come on, let's get some shut-eye."

I stood, walking silently behind this man I'd thought I knew so well.

Chapter 14

Darin was waiting outside the Whitefish Diner, squinting his eyes against the harsh afternoon sun. When he saw our van turn into the adjacent parking lot, he walked around back to meet us.

"Nick. Powers," Darin said, smiling. "How was your trip?"

Nick was out of the van in a flash.

"Smooth sailing, man." He gave his friend a hug. "Missed you, brother."

I got out and gave my old roommate a handshake and a pat on the back.

"Darin, man, it's great to see you. How's your mom doing?"

He grimaced.

"Well, you know. The same, really."

We piled into the van. Darin sat in the middle seat and directed us out of town to a heavily wooded section of northern Montana.

"This is how it's gonna go down," he explained. "We're going to park the van two miles outside of the Canadian border, and deliver the product by foot. Homeland Security has made a mess of trying to cross the borders through the gates. The guards can't be as easily paid off as they used to be. But don't worry, this is foolproof."

"Not a problem," Nick said, more to me. "We've done it this way dozens of times."

Darin continued, "The trail through the woods is painless. Two miles to the border and then two miles further, where I have a truck waiting. We'll be making several trips."

I nodded. A jittery feeling grew in my stomach, like border patrol was already watching us, camouflaged in the mountainous terrain. But the complete absence of cars and people on the narrow dirt road calmed my fears. All I saw in every direction was a never-ending sea of beautiful green.

The road was bumpy, and the few road signs we passed were riddled with holes from where the locals practiced their marksmanship.

"So," Darin said, "what gives with this delivery?"

Nick didn't respond.

"I mean," he continued, "why are we dropping off the product all the way up here?"

"What do you mean?" I asked.

Before Darin could answer, Nick cleared his throat and spoke. "I don't know. This is what I was told to do, so this is what we're doing. Simple as that. The Russians didn't care to elaborate, and I didn't care to ask questions."

"What are you guys talking about?"

"This delivery," Darin explained. "We've never made a drop-off in British Columbia, it's always the other way around. Nick and I have made pickups in British Columbia plenty of times, but never a drop-off. It's pennies on the dollar compared to the East Coast. We're losing money. That's what I don't get; why not sell to our normal contacts?"

"I really don't know." Agitation rolled across Nick's words. "I don't get it either. The Russians have worked with these guys in British Columbia many times, and so have we. So my only guess is that they want us to unload our supply to a mutual connection, to ensure that this goes down in the quickest manner possible."

Darin shook his head. "Doesn't sit right. It's bad business."

Nick turned sharply to him. "We do as we're told, and we get paid. Right?" His face was red, his weathered skin looking raw. My stomach felt queasy, and I had the sudden urge to be far away, back at home sitting around the fire pit with Becka.

The compacted dirt and pebble road got rougher, and after about a mile Darin pointed to the right.

"There. Pull over and I'll clear the way."

The van stopped and I jumped out with Darin, pulling aside a pile of branches that blended the driveway into the thicket bordering the side of the road. Nick turned the wheel and drove onto the property, slowly skirting the overgrown bushes and trees on either side. Darin and I resealed the entrance and followed the van until it drove onto a clearing with a small wooden shed in the center and a fire pit off to the side. Nick removed the keys, and the engine hissed and popped.

It was quiet out there, in a good way.

Darin went to the shed and opened the door. He went inside and started tossing large hiking backpacks on the ground. When he came out, he was carrying a case of bottled water.

"Okay," he said. "Suit up. There's still enough sunlight to make two, maybe three trips. It's four miles to our destination and four miles back."

He glanced at our shoes.

"Good thing you're both wearing sneakers."

Nick swung the back door of the van open and the sweet smell of marijuana hit my nostrils. Even with the product thoroughly wrapped and sealed, the smell was undeniable.

Darin grabbed a box and opened the lid. He removed a square package containing a pound of herb, put it to his nose, and then stuffed it in the bottom of his pack.

"Come on guys," he said. "Carry as much as you can."

Chapter 15

As the evening approached, we readied the campsite, collecting more than enough wood to burn through the night. It grew cold quickly out there in the mountains.

Nick came into the clearing carrying an armload of chopped branches.

"Another pile or two ought to do it," he said, dumping the logs on the pile. "Saw an old fell-over pine a ways up. Be back in a minute." He tested the sharpness of the axe blade with his thumb and walked back into the brush.

Darin was cleaning a cast-iron skillet with a cloth while I tended to the flame. I had used strips of the empty cardboard boxes—empty from the few deliveries we'd made before evening approached—to get the fire going.

I looked up to see Nick's faint outline blurred behind the dense underbrush and could hear the striking of his axe.

"What he'd tell you about these Russian guys?" I asked Darin.

Darin looked up from his work, placing the greasy cloth on a nearby rock. "Nothing, really. He called me in a rush, said he was leaving with a delivery. He explained that the operation had been bought out, but that's about it."

I nodded. "He told me some on the way here. These guys are ruthless. They threatened to kill him once."

"Yeah …" Darin cleared his throat. "I've heard some things. Look, I don't know if it's the best idea for us to trade notes, start speculating. Nick's still our boss. If he wants us knowing something, he'll tell us himself."

"True." I'd forgotten the first rule of management: *Keep your fucking mouth shut.*

Darin went and got our sleeping bags from the van as I tossed some more kindling on the growing fire. We were quiet for a bit, and then Darin asked, "He still scream in the middle of the night?"

"Not as often."

He nodded.

I wasn't about to ask if he knew about Frank White, or Mr. Carpenter X, but then Darin said, "Better off that guy is dead."

"So I hear."

Nick was still chopping at the tree, collecting more wood than we needed.

I cleared my throat and said, "Nick told me about you taking control of the operation … before this business with the Russians went down, that is."

Darin stopped unrolling a sleeping bag and looked up at me.

I continued, "I don't think we're speaking out of line when we're discussing our own futures."

Darin seemed to mull this over, and then said, "That was the plan. Nick's told me you'd have taken over the grow room when Jim retired. It would have been a smart move. You're a fast learner, Powers. We'd have made a good team."

"Maybe. Strange that Becka was never thought of. I mean, the girl's been working at the operation for as long as you have."

"Longer."

"Right. Longer."

"Don't know." Darin took a seat before the fire. "He keeps her at arm's reach. Just close enough to stay busy, but far enough away to not be involved in anything serious. Nick's known her since she was a teenager; he probably still sees her as a little girl. She pissed about you becoming management?"

"You could say that. She's indirect, but I know she's pissed. Even more pissed that I'm out here making this run. I think she's jealous, or maybe overprotective. I don't know."

"Shit." Darin laughed, looking around the woods. "She could take my place out here. This is the last delivery. No pride comes from this."

"True enough."

Darin placed the skillet on a flat rock at the base of the flames, using a stick to spread the bright coals around the stone.

"Well," he said, looking at a lineup of canned food. "We got chili and we got chili. What'll it be?"

"I'll take the steak."

He laughed.

"In all seriousness," I asked, "and you don't have to answer if you don't want to … how is your mother?"

His smile vanished as he began opening the cans.

"A few weeks, maybe. They originally gave her til April, but we've passed that mark, so who knows."

"You staying here … after?"

Darin shook his head.

"Don't know. It will take a while to settle her affairs. I'll probably come back east to the Barrens. There's nothing much for me here."

"Well, it will be good having you at the house again. We could use a set of hands in the garden."

He smiled.

"You're good at making light of things, Powers."

Nick came back into the clearing with an armload of sappy yet dry pine branches and dumped them on the woodpile. He wiped his sweaty forehead with his back of his hand.

"That's it. That's enough." He pulled a cigarette from the pack with his teeth. "What are you guys chatting about?"

"Nothing," I said. "Ready to eat?"

"Damn straight."

***

That night we slept under the stars.

Nick woke earlier than Darin and me, and re-lit the smoldering campfire. He was trying to stifle back his morning coughs, but the noise woke me up despite his efforts.

"Morning, Nick." I sat up in my sleeping bag.

"I wake you?"

I shook my head. "No," I lied.

Darin was moving about in his sleeping bag, clearly awake but not willing to get up.

A kettle of water was heating over the flames, and when steam began to issue, Nick filled our tin cups with the near-boiling water and added a scoop of instant coffee.

Nick blew back the vapors and took a sip. "Not bad, considering."

I sipped at the rim of the tin cup, the metal just as scalding as the coffee inside. I wanted to say, "Tastes like crap," but I said, "Yeah, not bad."

Darin got up a few minutes later, rubbing the sleep from his eyes.

"Let's eat," he said after a yawn. "We got a lot of walking to do today."

The previous evening we had made two trips across the border. The hike was relatively easy, and would have been quite beautiful if my mind hadn't been swimming with worry. By the time we got back to the van after the second trip, we had walked roughly sixteen miles and my legs were much sorer than I cared to admit.

"How many trips you think are left?" I asked.

Darin stood, stretching his back, and looked off toward the van as if he could approximate the amount of product left to deliver just by observing the rear door.

He wrinkled his forehead. "Don't know. Maybe six trips? Not sure."

I gulped.

***

My legs were no longer sore—they felt broken, the muscles and tendons ripped to shreds, torn in half. The three of us had been walking in the woods all morning and afternoon.

It was early evening now … and we were done. Finished. The last bricks of marijuana were stacked in the back of the van on the Canadian border. The three of us sat in the front seat, sweat soaked, dirty, and exhausted. Darin drove, dropping me off in a town named Nelson while he and Nick went to deliver the product.

Standing on the side of the road, my few meager possessions stuffed in my duffle bag, a wave of relief overtook me as I watched the drugs drive off without me. My accumulated stress began to ebb, making even the pain in my legs all the more tolerable. Pleasant almost. Like I'd just finished running a marathon on a windy day.

Down the block, I checked into the hostel that Darin pointed out, securing a private room containing two bunk beds and nothing more. The communal bathroom was down the hallway. The guy at the counter took American currency, and when I told him Darin Long was with me, he didn't ask for a passport or driver's license.

Walking toward the downtown, I admired the vibrant homes and businesses in this artistic mountain town. I found the place we'd agreed to meet, a bar called Temple Bar, a cross between an Irish pub, a Western joint, and something like a club. It was strange. A DJ table was set up by the dance floor, cranking out a mix of Creedence Clearwater, Bob Marley, and mindless dance music. Most of the clientele looming about the place looked entirely too stoned to think about dancing. A few natives with long, thick dreadlocks came and went, and several middle-aged drifters sat around a table, drunk on the local porter and smelling strongly of stale cigarettes and filth.

I stared absentmindedly at the bar counter, unable to move from my seat. My legs now felt like cement as the first beer coursed through my veins. I could smell myself: a mixture of campfire and sweat. I smelled like a man, the way a man should smell. My jeans and shirt hadn't been changed in two days, and they felt a part of my skin.

The front door opened and closed as I was ordering my second porter, and a flash of streetlight illuminated the dark interior. Nick and Darin walked into the barroom.

When they were within earshot, I said, "Well?"

Nick smiled. "I need a beer."

"All is good, Powers," Darin said, patting my shoulder. "All is good."

Another flood of relief washed over me, aided by the numbing effect of the alcohol on my worn muscles.

The bartender walked over, resting his thick palms on the counter.

Nick smiled at the man. "How's your day going?"

The man shrugged. "What'll it be?"

"Pale ale. Sierra Nevada if you got it, or whatever's local." His eyes scanned the taps for a Sierra Nevada handle. "Two of them please." He pointed between himself and Darin, placing a twenty down on the bar. "And a third when he's ready."

The bartender dropped off the beers, made change of the twenty, and the three of us clinked glasses. We didn't say a word about what we had just accomplished, and we didn't have to. Three things went through our minds as if we were speaking with telepathy:

1. The last of our product was delivered, out of our hands.
2. We were free of the Russians.
3. Nick could finally retire.

Yes, Nick Grady was free—free of his monstrous old partner, Frank White. He was out of the business for good. Despite that I was now unemployed, I was glad that my friend could finally be at peace.

We ordered another round, along with some whiskey, and we drank it all in a matter of minutes. The dark liquor went down like water and heated my stomach—a very pleasant sensation.

We moved to a private table and asked for menus, though we already knew we'd be ordering the largest, bloodiest, slabs of meat that the place carried.

The steaks came out charred on top, cooked fast on a hot flame. For ten minutes we didn't speak, but devoured the life-giving meat, chewing huge mouthfuls and feeling the hot juices run down our throats. I added butter and salt to my baked potato, and fork-mashed it against the plate to sop up any remaining juices. When we'd finished, nothing edible was left on our plates, and we had devoured two baskets of bread.

We washed the meal down with a shot of whiskey and ordered another round before the waitress had finished clearing our plates.

"Thirsty, huh?" she said with a grin.

"Parched," Nick replied. "Grab a shot for yourself, if you're allowed."

She seemed to contemplate his offer, and then came back cheering along with us.

It didn't take long for my vision to begin to blur and the music to start sounding better and better. The bar crowd grew as the night wore on, and I was happy to see life being enjoyed. People were now on the dance floor, mostly young transient chicks who danced like primal beings, their beads and dreadlocks bouncing on their shoulders. They danced with a passion, their movements making the music a thing alive. They danced with their souls on fire.

Nick's face was aglow, and his body seemed to want to join them on the dance floor, but I imagined his aching muscles kept him seated.

It grew late. Our spirits were high and the booze flowed. Suddenly the lights in the bar turned up. I looked at Nick with a shocked expression.

"Closing time?"

He checked his watch and shrugged. "Guess so."

We stumbled outside. The walk to the hostel was short, but we took our time to chain-smoke cigarettes and talk way too loud for this quiet town at night.

Back in our room, we closed the door and collapsed on the beds. I took the top bunk, and Darin took the one beneath me. Nick sat alone across the short hallway and kicked off his shoes in a slow and drunken manner. I wasn't going to bother taking my clothing off at all, except for my shoes. Tomorrow I would shower and change. At the moment, the room was spinning ever so slightly. Total exhaustion was close at hand.

"So," Nick said. "Tomorrow, we go back to the van and head home."

"Amen," Darin said.

Nick cleared his throat, and spoke in a near whisper. "I think it's time ... I told you more about these guys. The Russians."

He paused, and in the silence my hearing perked up.

Nick scooted closer to the window and lit a cigarette, blowing the smoke outside and waving it away with his hand.

"The Russians are how I met my partner, Carpenter X. It started back when I was only a teenager ..."

Chapter 16

Summer, 1967

"Turn that shit down, would ya?"

Young Nick Grady turned to the television and spun the volume dial down a notch. *The Monkees* had just started, and the theme song echoed loud in the small apartment. Nick's roommate Dennis got up from the table and turned the channel knob.

"Can't stand this shit," he said.

Nick's other roommate, Pete, turned to Dennis. "What? *The Monkees?*"

"Yeah, *The Monkees.*"

Pete shook his head and went back to work sorting the mounds of marijuana piled high on the table into weighted bags. Nick didn't look up from the scale as he listened to the channels click and then stop on a news station. A newscaster was talking about the increased troop presence in Vietnam, and grainy clips of soldiers trudging through dense forests flashed on the screen. Dennis clicked the TV off. They were all eligible for the draft, and rumors of a lottery were rampant.

Dennis went through a stack of records in a milk crate, flipping from one to another. After a minute, Nick heard the needle of the record player scratch and then the melodious harmonica of Bob Dylan bellowed from the speakers.

They spent the rest of the afternoon packaging their product, getting high, and listening to records. It had been four months since Vitali, Nikolay, and their men kicked in the door, and Nick and his two roommates had slowly regained their sense of security.

They had been working for the organization ever since that fateful day when they were left shaking and cowering on the cold dirt of the woods as the van sped away, their minds in a panic, their nerves scrambled, and their hands still tied behind their backs. But time had passed, and they continued to work. Fortunately for them, Vitali and Nikolay showed a more pleasant side when the product came in on schedule and money exchanged hands. The Russians paid them fairly, treating them like business partners, and not like slaves. They even taught the three of them some conversational Russian, and Nick was getting the hang of it.

The roommates were now making more money working for the Russians than they ever would have on their own.

Pete called out through the wailing of Bob Dylan, "What time you got?"

Nick checked his watch. "Three thirty."

"All right," Pete said, lighting up a joint the size of his thumb. "We got an hour, so let's get to it."

Dennis took the joint from Pete. "Chill, man. We got time."

They continued to weigh and package their product, stacking the individual brick-sized bags into large cardboard boxes until the weed on the table was down to scrapings. What was left was theirs.

"I'll pull the van around," Dennis said, checking his watch. "We gotta book it."

Dennis got up and grabbed his denim jacket from the couch. Nick and Pete followed, looking for their coats. Pete went to the desk in the room and put a key in the top drawer. He fumbled inside and pulled out a small Smith and Wesson .38 revolver. He tucked the pistol in his belt between his front and rear pockets and pulled his coat over to cover.

Nick shook his head. "You don't need that shit."

"Nick, man, I ain't taking any chances. We got to protect our interests. If something happens on the way to the drop-off, Vitali and Nikolay will have our balls. Not to mention that we still can't trust these guys, these Russians. I ain't never gonna let them threaten me like they did that day."

Nick shook his head. "If Vitali finds out you're carrying—"

"Vitali ain't gonna find out, you dig? It's 'cause of him I got it. I'm protecting *his* interests."

"Just keep it in the van."

Pete didn't respond. Dennis went to the door, grabbing his keys off the kitchen counter. He paused at the desk and reached inside the drawer for his Colt .45 automatic. The pistol was his father's, brought home from when he served in France.

Nick was about to say something, but he knew it would fall on deaf ears. Pete had started carrying a piece two weeks ago, and Dennis soon followed. It was pointless, Nick thought, but the guys were adamant about their protection. They were big-time now, they said. No more bullshit. They would fight back if anyone tried to shake them down. They would stand their ground. That's what real gangsters did, they said. That's how this business works, they said.

Nick wasn't so sure.

"Hurry up and get the van." Pete straightened his coat. "We gotta fly."

Dennis left and backed the van into the driveway. They loaded the boxes into the trunk and sped off.

Vitali and Nikolay's warehouse was across town, south of the main highway. Dennis drove to the loading dock and came to a stop. Pete opened the passenger door and got out. He walked to a side entrance beside the sliding garage door and knocked. A minute later, the garage door began to squeal open, and Pete came jogging back to the van.

"Let's go," he said, closing the passenger door.

Dennis put the van in reverse and slowly backed up against the cargo bay.

Pete and Dennis got out, and Nick followed. The warehouse went back an unseen distance, with racks upon racks of boxes and crates piled high. The squealing sound of a forklift, its engine rumbling, vibrated across the cavernous room.

Four men came out of a side office. Vitali and Nikolay stood in the middle.

"Boys, boys," Vitali said, palms outward. "Right on time."

Men began removing the boxes from the rear of the van, inspecting the contents, and weighing the stock on a floor-mounted scale. The two men on either side of Vitali and Nikolay towered tall above their bosses, wearing suits with open collars, cool as could be. Pump-action shotguns hung from shoulder slings, their palms resting on the straps. More armed men were nearby.

Vitali asked, "How is the harvest doing, hmm?"

"Good," Pete said. "The next delivery will be on schedule."

"That's good, boys. That's very good."

The rear door of the van was closed and the sliding garage door squealed shut. A man walked to Vitali, holding a paper indicating the weight and amount of product. Vitali spoke to the man in Russian, and the man went off toward the office. Nick tried to piece together their conversation, but they spoke entirely too fast for him to comprehend.

In the man's absence, everyone fell into silence. The guard straight across from Nick was chewing on a toothpick, his massive palm leisurely gripping his shotgun strap. His jaw protruded like stone and his dark eyes scanned over Nick and his roommates.

Finally, the man came back from the office passing a manila envelope to Vitali.

"This should be to your liking, no?" Vitali passed the envelope across to Pete, who stood in the middle between Nick and Dennis.

What happened next occurred in the blink of an eye, yet each fraction of a second became ingrained in Nick's memory like photographs. Nick saw Pete take the envelope in his left hand. At the same time, Pete moved his jacket back with his right hand to tuck the money in the rear pocket of his pants … but he never got that far.

The dark eyes of the man standing across from Nick flashed wide and his mouth hung open, the toothpick stuck to his bottom lip. Nick's eyes followed the man's gaze to Pete's side where the handle of the .38 jutted out from his belt, his fingers skirting dangerously close to the handle. By the time Nick's eyes darted back to the man across from him, the guard had already swung his shotgun into his hands in a well-practiced movement.

The shotgun was loaded and ready to fire.

The man pulled the trigger.

Pete's body flew backwards and the entire room seemed to recoil from the sound of the blast. Nick flung himself to his side behind a stack of boxes, and Dennis ducked and sought cover as bullets erupted out of nowhere, striking the concrete floor and pelting the metal walls behind them.

"Oh shit!" Nick screamed, covering his ears and keeping his forehead against the cold ground. "Shit-shit-shit-shit!"

Dennis pulled his pistol and shot the man who had killed Pete, and as he ducked to his side, he aimed at the other guard and fired. Vitali and Nikolay had vanished.

Tiny fragments of cement pelted Nick's face and forearms as he crouched low against the ground, and he crawled backwards, making a desperate scramble toward the door by the sliding cargo bay. In a flash, he got up and ran.

Nick burst outside, not sure which way was which. The sound of bullet fire hitting the metal sliding door behind him made him cower. Nick patted his pockets and dug for his keys with his shaking hand. He ran around to the driver's side of his van, his keys clenched between his fingers, and then he came to a sudden grinding halt. Red handprints smeared the white side of the van. A trickle of blood trailed back to the side of the warehouse. One of the guards lay slumped over, his back against the van and his hand clutching the side of his abdomen. A shotgun was clutched in his palm.

He looked up at Nick and swung the shotgun straight into his face. Nick's eyes went large.

Nick raised his hands in surrender, the keys jingling in his fingers.

The man closed his eyes and let out a long breath.

"Kid," he said in a huff as he lifted his shirt and dug for something in his pocket, "get me out of here." Nick looked down at a bleeding hole that went straight through the man's lower left side. Above the wound was a bulletproof vest with a second bullet lodged over his stomach. But Nick barely noticed. His gaze focused on the shining badge smeared red that the undercover officer held in his hand.

"Get me out of here," the man said in labored breaths, "and I'll get you off the hook, scot-free … just get me out of here."

Just then, two men ran around the corner of the warehouse from the front gate, pistols drawn. They stopped short when they saw Vitali's guard shot and bleeding, with a pale and terrified Nick hovering above him.

"I-inside," the man said. "Get i-in there, they need your help. Now!"

The men ran to the door.

As soon as the door closed behind the guards, Nick turned back to the man on the ground. "My friends …"

"They're dead," he said. "Listen."

The air was quiet. The popping of gunfire had ceased.

"You got about t-two seconds before they come bursting back through that d-door. What's it gonna be, kid?"

Chapter 17

Nick dropped his finished cigarette in the empty beer bottle and swirled it around with the other bloated butts that he'd chain-smoked.

I felt entirely more sober.

"So," I said from my top bunk. "That's how you met your partner?"

Nick nodded. "Saved his life. Carpenter X, his name was Frank White. There were two other cops who worked with Frank back then, each as corrupt as the next: Richard Barrett and Martin Brady."

Darin cleared his throat. "Nick, I had no idea. That's ... crazy. My God. What happened after you found him shot?"

Nick lit another cigarette and took a sip from a flask-sized bottle of Jack.

"I sped the hell out of there with Frank bleeding all over the van. He went real pale; I thought he was gonna die right there in the passenger seat. Would have been better off if he had." Nick spat a loose piece of tobacco off his lip.

"He made you work for him?" Darin asked. "Did he have his own operation going? Is that why he was infiltrating the Russians?"

Nick shook his head. "Frank infiltrated Vitali because he was working in narcotics. But him and those two scumbags, Richard and Martin, they were making money on the side, controlling a few small-time dealers. Once they got you, they never let go. They had you by the balls for the rest of your life, either through blackmail or physical abuse. I was forced to stay in business, giving them half the profits."

"At least they kept the Russians off your back, right?" Darin offered.

Nick shot him a fierce look. "Would have rather faced the Russians. Those fuckers killed my roommates, nearly killed me. I tried to find out what happened to Pete's and Dennis's bodies, but Frank always told me to forget about it. Thinking about them decaying in the woods, or chopped up in pieces, or dissolved in acid ..."

Nick went back to smoking, and Darin and I tried to exchange quick glances, but I was sitting on the bunk right above him. We waited for Nick to elaborate, but he didn't.

"So, Frank got you off the hook somehow?"

Nick nodded. "You could say that. Richard and Martin brought me to the station after I got Frank to the hospital. They took me to a room in the basement." Nick took a pull from the bottle. "They ..." Nick shook his head. "It doesn't matter, none of this matters. It's old news. They're dead, all of them, and I'm still alive. They can rot in hell for all of eternity."

He took another swig, and Darin reached across the bunks asking for a drink, mostly just to keep the bottle away from Nick. He was getting that look, that faraway gaze that could splinter into one of his drunken rambles.

Darin took a drink and handed me up the bourbon. I took a large pull, trying to drain as much as I could before handing it back to Nick.

But surprisingly, Nick finished his cigarette and stood up on wobbly legs to go use the bathroom. He turned by the doorway and said, "Let's get some shut-eye. We got a long walk back to the van tomorrow."

When he was gone, I looked under my bunk to Darin below.

"Damn," I said.

"Yeah, ain't that some shit? I can't believe he kept that secret for so long."

"At least he's talking now."

"Maybe." Darin yawned, shaking his head. "But maybe we'd be better off not knowing."

***

The hike back to the van was harder than I'd anticipated. My legs felt like jelly at times, and like cement at others. The bottoms of my feet were hot with blisters and seemed to be yelling at me to stop—*Stop right there! Sit the fuck down!*

To top it off, my hangover was a bitch.

Darin's and Nick's must have been too.

We first stopped for a big breakfast of scrambled eggs, thick pancakes with gobs of butter and syrup, bacon, sausages so loaded with fat that they burst with juices when cut, and toast loaded with even more butter. It helped, a little. Coffee helped more, along with aspirin, orange juice, and water. Lots of water. We drank more water as we hiked the unmarked trail, stopping often to urinate against massive fir trees.

Once we passed the invisible US border, we began talking more boldly, remembering that we no longer had a van full of drugs to worry about. We were free men. Nick and I even discussed making some stops along the way home, hit up a few national parks. Yellowstone, the Grand Tetons, maybe the Badlands.

My hangover was ebbing when we saw a familiar stream cutting through dense foliage, telling us that we were nearing our van. We stopped to splash the crystal-clear water on our faces, washing away the alcohol-infused sweat that the hike was helping us to shed.

Darin was saying, "If I were you guys, I would stay in Missoula tonight. I'm surprised you didn't stop on your way here. It's a cool town, lots of breweries—"

Nick froze and waved him quiet, dropping to a knee and peering through the brush. Darin and I did the same, looking off into the woods.

Our van was right there, just a few yards away. It was parked in the clearing, just as we'd left it. Only, there were several people walking around it. Once we quieted and I focused my hearing, I could make out the grumbling of words, impossible to decipher.

Nick looked back at me and swallowed. They were speaking Russian.

Chapter 18

It was clear that they had seen us and we had seen them. The four men spoke in whispers, standing shoulder to shoulder, staring in our direction.

Nick stood exposed from the brush and began walking in their direction.

"*Nick*," Darin hissed. "Nick, you sure about this? *Nick?*"

Nick walked forward and we stood and followed, staying several feet behind.

As we neared I could see the men more clearly. The young guy on the far left was the tall fuck from the warehouse, and the one on the right was the shorter fuck who had waved a gun in my face. They both wore jeans with baseball hats that looked brand new and said "Montana" on them. The two older men in the middle wore suits with open collars that looked odd in juxtaposition to the wilderness.

One of the older men cracked a grin and brushed a palm over his obviously dyed black hair.

When we got within earshot, the man took a step forward.

"Nick," his voice bellowed in a worn Russian accent. "Hope you have enjoyed the exercise and the beauty of the wilderness." He stood with arms open wide, looking absently at the treetops above. "Such clean air, no?"

Nick stared at him.

"And you, Mr. Darin and Mr. Evan, such a pleasure it is to finally meet you. I've been keeping a fond eye on you both."

My eyes twitched as I fought the urge to exchange glances with Darin.

Nick said, "What are you doing here?"

The man soured his expression, feigning resentment, and looked at the other older gentleman beside him.

"Why the hostility? Do you not want to be paid for your troubles?"

The man motioned to his guard, and the big man stepped forward, handing his boss a duffel bag with a large Nike symbol stretching the side. The older man offered it out by the straps, but Nick didn't budge.

"There's a little something extra in there for you." The man tossed the duffel bag to Nick's feet.

"A retirement present?" Nick smirked.

"Retirement?" The man shook his head slowly. "You are way too valuable of an employee to quit now."

I swallowed back a rising lump in my throat as sweat droplets formed on my face.

The man began talking in Russian to his company when Nick cut in, speaking Russian along with them. I looked at Darin and he looked at me. Nick's sentences sounded slow and choppy, but we still couldn't understand a word of what he said.

After a short exchange back and forth, the well-dressed man on the right stepped forward, pulled a small piece of paper from his jacket pocket, and handed it to Nick. Nick looked down at the note as the men continued speaking. He slipped the paper in his pocket, and they finally began speaking in English again.

"It's a down payment," the Russian said, pointing to the duffel bag.

"For what?" Nick stammered. "You gave me your word. I'm done, through ..."

"It's a down payment for your next assignment. Deliver the four kilograms of cocaine that we had the decency of securing in your van for you."

Nick shook his head. I couldn't see his face from where I stood, but I was certain his eyes were huge.

"I'm done, I'm—"

"You can be done," the words escaped the man's mouth in a hiss, the smile gone from his face, "when you are resting as calmly as your old partner, Mr. Frank White. Until then, you owe your loyalty to me; to our organization."

The man's cheeks turned a crimson red. "You swore your allegiance to us all of those years ago, and then you went to work with the enemy—the *police.*"

"I didn't have a choice. You know this. And those men were hardly police. They had you in their pockets just as much as they had me."

The man took a breath, his smirk returning ever so slyly.

"Whatever the case," he said, "you are still a member of my organization. You are *all* members of my organization." The man made eye contact with Darin and myself. "We own your company and your lives. You work for me, and as a matter of goodwill, I have delivered to you an advance payment for your next assignment. Each kilogram of cocaine has a value of, say, twenty thousand dollars wholesale. Once cut, each kilo will triple in street value. Of course, that depends on market trends and the sizes of the bags. One kilo cuts down to one thousand individual grams, each selling for sixty dollars. You can do the math, see how important this job is to me—how important it is to *you.* We are not discussing trivial matters, now are we?"

No one said a word.

I thought back to our conversation a few days ago about the marijuana delivery. Why were we up there, delivering our product for a much lower profit when we could have sold it locally for a much higher percentage? It was all a ruse. The Russians didn't care about selling the pot … they wanted to get us closer to the cocaine.

Nick shook his head. "I don't sell this shit. You know that. I never have and I never will. It's off the menu."

"I'm not asking you to sell it; I am telling you to deliver it. Drug mules, I think it is called, no?"

The men in jeans stifled a laugh, adjusting their clasped hands before them. I had no delusion that these men weren't armed.

"Well," the man said, turning his back, "I leave it in your hands. Darin, I know you live here in this desolate shithole of a state, so you may remain behind. I will contact you in the coming months when the next delivery is ready for transport. This first shipment is relatively small. Just a trial, if you will."

With that, the men walked across the grassy enclosure toward their Cadillac.

Nick called after them. "We don't swing this shit!"

They paused, and one of the well-dressed men shouted back. "We left a map for you in the van, with the drop-off location circled. It is close to your home. Have a safe trip." He ducked inside the car and closed the door. The Cadillac backed out of the clearing, leaving the three of us darting our eyes between the duffel bag and the van like they were things poisoned.

"Nick." My voice croaked. "What are we going to do?"

Chapter 19

The van seemed to be weighed down by the load, running sluggishly. This was purely in my head, of course.

We were a long way from home, traveling through Whitefish, Montana, where we dropped Darin off in front of his house.

"The one on the left, who did most of the talking, that was Vitali. The one on the right was his brother, Nikolay," Nick informed me.

I didn't care who was who at that moment. They both looked the same, nearly identical.

"Nick," I said. "What are we going to do?" I envisioned my life now, a pack mule for drug kingpins. It was absurd, out of the question. How did this happen? Not long ago, I was working days in the office and spending my evenings listening to music, drinking beer, and working part time for Nick at the warehouse. But that was different; all I did was weigh some pot on a scale and put it in bags. It was harmless. It was fun. A party every night, and regular sex with a girl that I was practically dating. The people at Nick's warehouse were happy, almost childlike at times. I envisioned Jim Hoffman dancing around the plants with his earphone cords dangling, lost in his work, humming and singing out loud to his inaudible music.

Nick nervously tapped the steering wheel. I couldn't decipher if his straight-ahead gaze and clenched jaw indicated he was shocked or angry. Probably both.

"Powers, man ... I don't know. I just don't know."

His voice was weak.

"All right, all right." I paused to think. I had to put myself in Nick's shoes. The guy had been working in the drug business for decades, and from what I had recently found out, it was not completely by choice. Maybe at the beginning it was. He had always seemed happy, but along the way he had dealt with some serious hardships. The man had witnessed his friends getting killed. He was forced into the business, first with gangsters, and then with crooked cops who abused him in some god-awful way that I still didn't know much about. Now a middle-aged man, he had thought he was free. But Vitali and Nikolay had not forgiven him for the shoot-out in their warehouse all those years ago.

And it seemed that they never would.

"They don't really need us," I said. "Vitali and Nikolay, they're only doing this to get revenge on you."

Nick didn't respond.

"Maybe this is it, maybe they're just toying with us. We make this delivery and we're off the hook."

"No." Nick shook his head. "That's not the way they do business. They corrupt people through intimidation and reward." Nick pointed to the duffel bag by my feet. We'd only opened the zipper and looked inside at the stacks of money. For some reason, we didn't touch the bills, almost afraid that the money would be hot to the touch. "It's the same method they used when I was a teenager. They're threatening us, and yet paying us handsomely. They want us to want to work for them, yet always be too afraid to leave. We're dogs," Nick continued. "They treat people like dogs. Do what they say, get a cookie. Disobey, get the whip."

I gulped. I wanted to shout out, *What are we going to do? Nick!* but it was pointless. Nick didn't know, and if he did, he wasn't inclined to tell me at the moment. I knew the gears of his mind were working, grinding away, and that something of a plan must be forming. At least I hoped so, because I was terrified beyond rational thought.

"What were you guys talking about in Russian?"

I heard him swallow, but he remained quiet.

"What did he give you?" I asked.

"What?"

"That paper. What was it?"

Nick shook his head. "Something … personal. Something that has nothing to do with this predicament."

"Nick, I think *everything* now pertains to this predicament."

Nick shot me a sideways glance.

"Powers, just give me some time. Okay? Let me think things through. I need a few hours—a day or two. I'll figure it out, I swear."

I wanted to believe that he was right.

"We gotta call Becka, give her a heads-up."

"No." His voice was stern. "Don't call her. Don't mention her name around the Russians, or anybody for that matter. She knows to stay away, and that's exactly what she needs to do. Got it?"

"Yeah, but don't you think—"

"Listen to me, Powers. Keep your distance. I know you guys have a thing, whatever it is, but you stay the fuck away from her for a while. You know she's strong-headed. If she thinks we're in trouble, she might go off and do something stupid like try to help. The best thing to do is leave her alone. Don't contact her. Don't contact *anyone* from the operation. You understand?"

I wasn't so sure he was right. Keeping my distance was going to be hard, nearly impossible. All I wanted to do since our last phone conversation was hear her voice, spend a night holding her tight against my chest, smelling that special spot on the top of her head that keeps a person's true scent all throughout their lifetime, from birth to death. But Nick might be right. The thought that something could happen to her, that I could be responsible for causing her harm, was a serious concern.

"Powers," Nick said sharply, then, over-pronouncing his words. "Do-you-understand?"

"Yes," I answered. "I understand. I'll keep my distance."

***

The last time I had showered was at the hostel in British Columbia, and the feeling of the jets of hot water stripping away the several-days' layer of grime on my body was amazing. However, it was far easier walking around smelling strongly of campfire with a week-old beard in this part of the country. In New Jersey or New York, people would look at me like I just committed a crime. Out here in the West, nobody batted an eye when they saw what looked like two guys coming back from a fishing trip.

We stopped at The Cartwheel Inn, just one full day's drive away from home. For the past hour I had been in the bathroom. First, I soaked in the tub until the water turned a murky brown. Then I showered, just standing under the jets of water, letting the steamy heat permeate my body. I don't know how long I stood there, but when I was finished, and had scrubbed my skin raw, I stepped out of the hazy bathroom and into an empty room. Nick had left to find us food.

Once dressed, I sipped at a beer until I heard movement by the door. Nick came walking in.

"Beer?" I asked, as he closed the door behind him.

He nodded and took a bottle, his face sweaty from the walk.

I looked at his hands. "Where's the food?"

He opened his palms in exasperation.

"Nothing's open." He took a long swig. "Not one goddamn store open in all of this shithole town."

"Well, we have a half bag of pretzels in the van."

Nick drained back the beer.

"Have at it." He took another bottle and popped off the cap using his lighter. "I'm taking a shower. A long one."

Nick took the beer into the bathroom, and a moment later I heard the water running.

During the first leg of our trip we spoke at length about what we were going to do, how we were going to get out of our predicament. Only, we couldn't find a solution. Constantly worrying about the enormous amount of cocaine secured under a tarp in the van made our nerves shot, our minds erratic.

For the past day we had barely spoken. The stress of the situation was becoming debilitating. All I could think about was how great my life had been only a week ago. At home, the garden would be glistening in the moonlight, and I longed to be sipping a beer beside it.

***

The traffic got worse closer to the East Coast. We were now only hours away from home, driving bumper-to-bumper in rush-hour traffic. The sun would be setting shortly, but the sky was breathtaking at the moment.

"Nick," I said, lowering the music. "We need to talk. We got to figure things out. Are we just going to make the drop and go on working for these guys?"

Nick took a long wind of air. He had been quiet all day. More so than usual.

"Look," he said, wiping his forehead on his arm. His cheeks were flushed. "I've been doing some thinking …"

There was a pause.

I was about to say, "What? *What were you thinking?* Spit it out!" but then Nick continued. "I've worked things out, okay? You need to listen to me carefully and not ask any questions."

He looked to me, taking his gaze momentarily off the road. His eyes were red and swollen, yet they radiated something odd. They shone with an unsettling intensity.

Chapter 20

"What? No way, Nick!"

"You promised you'd do as I said and not ask any questions."

"No, actually, I didn't."

He didn't respond.

"I don't get it," I continued. "How is that going to get us off the hook?"

"Trust me. You have to trust me. I already talked to Rob, it's a done deal."

I was speechless. When had Nick talked to our landlord?

"I called him from a pay phone, yesterday." He seemed to have guessed my thoughts. "While you were showering."

"You've known this since yesterday and waited until now to tell me?"

Nick sighed. "Okay, okay. Let's talk about this rationally. Vitali and Nikolay, they don't care about you or Darin. Sorry, but that's true. You can get out of this. You *are* getting out of this."

"And what about you?"

"I have a plan."

"Yeah, a plan that you don't want to share with me."

I turned from him, looking out the window.

"Powers, man, you just got to trust me. Please." There was a longing in his voice, a desperate tone.

"So," I said, rubbing my temples, "you're going to drop me off at home, tonight. You want me to pack my stuff and leave. Split town."

"It's the only thing we can do," Nick said. "Rob will let us out of the lease. We have to pay him two months' rent, and I have to turn over the garden and put down grass seed. That ground is actually part of the park system, and wasn't supposed to be built upon. It's conserved land. Whatever you don't pack is going to the curb Monday morning, so don't leave anything important behind. I've thought long and hard about the best course of action, and this is it. If you take off now, before the Russians invest much stock in you, there's a good chance they won't look far to track you down. I'm the one they want. Besides, I don't think their organization has the same reach as it used to. So far, I've only seen the same handful of men. They are desperate to rebuild their operation, and that's why they're forcing us to work for them. I think they need us to make this delivery, because they don't have anyone else to do it. Why force people to work for you? It's risky. Bad business. You leaving town is safer than giving up, handing over your life for these guys to ruin. Trust me. Take your share of the money and run."

"Run where?"

"Anywhere. I don't know. Go somewhere warm. Florida, Mexico. There's enough money in your cut to see you off safely. You'll have to work again, but not for a while."

"What about Darin?"

Nick cleared his throat. "I'll call him tonight. I'll wire him some money and make sure he also leaves town."

"And you?"

"I'm leaving too. I'll drop off their drugs, turn over the soil in the garden, and disappear."

"Disappear where?"

He glanced at me, then back to the road.

"Powers." He sighed. "This is the end of the road for us. You can't know where I'm going, and I don't want to know where you're going. We have to split up and go our separate ways."

I shook my head, trying to figure out Nick's angle. How was he going to escape Vitali and his crew? It was likely that Nick didn't have a plan at all. It was likely that Nick was going to make the drop and then continue working for these guys, sacrifice himself so that the rest of us could get out safely.

"I don't like it." I stared out the window.

"You don't have to like it," Nick said, lighting a cigarette. "But you're doing it."

We were quiet for a few minutes, listening to the wind whizz by the van.

"Here," Nick said. "I want to show you something."

He dug in his pocket and removed a wrinkled Polaroid photograph.

"What's this?" I looked down at the picture. "Jesus Christ, is that you?"

Nick nodded. "That's what Vitali gave me in the woods. It wasn't a note."

I looked at the picture in my hands. It was old, grainy and blurred. I saw Nick as a boy, a teenager, just the top of his bare shoulders and head. His face was battered, his eyes swollen shut, with stitches running over his forehead and cheekbones. I had always noticed minor scars on Nick's face, but they were so light that they seemed to belong to his weathered skin.

"What the hell happened?"

Nick paused, took a deep breath, then started talking. "Richard Barrett and Martin Brady, the two cops. They are what happened. When I rushed Frank to the hospital, Richard and Martin were waiting for me by the sliding glass door to the emergency room. Richard took me to their cruiser while Martin parked my blood-soaked van somewhere safe. They said everything was going to be all right. They said I did a good job, saved their friend. They said I was a hero. They told me I was safe; everything was going to work out. We drove to the station, and I remember seeing a dozen or so people, kids really, protesting the war outside Borough Hall. Some were even burning their draft cards. I felt sorry for them, like they were in a worse place in life than myself." Nick took a deep breath, and then continued. "They took me to the station, to a side door. It was quiet, I remember. Just a few cops here and there, sitting at desks, talking on phones and doing paperwork. They took me to a staircase in the back, and then one of them put his hand on my shoulder. His grip was tight. They stopped talking, but guided me onward down the stairs. There was no one else down there, just a few rooms. Storage, I guess. They pushed me through a doorway in the back … and locked the door behind them. They took out their batons and hit my legs. They kicked me when I fell, and continued whacking me with their nightsticks and gloved fists. I'm sure I was yelling out, screaming, but for the life of me I can't remember a word I said. Eventually they scooped me up. My blood stung my eyes, so hot like it couldn't have come from my body. There was a great wooden round table in the center of the room. The chairs fell over, scattered from my beating. They slammed me on top of the table … and …" He took another deep breath. "… beat me unconscious. When I woke up, I was in the corner of the room, freezing cold on the cement floor. The room was silent. I couldn't move, and I drifted in and out of dazed sleep. Some time later, they brought me a glass of water and told me to stand up. I wasn't sure if I could, but they made me stand anyway. Things in my body cracked and popped, and they shoved me along to the staircase. A car waited outside. They told me that I belonged to them, and they could do whatever they wanted to me. I was their property, and I was ordered to work for them. If I tried to fight back, I would be locked up for the attempted murder of Officer Frank White."

Nick was silent for a moment, and I thought he was done. I was racking my brain for something to say, but then he continued. "The officer named Martin, he had a wife and kids. He only beat me that one time. But that sick fuck Richard, he showed up at my front door plenty of times just to give me a wallop. I couldn't do anything. Fighting back was out of the question. I had to take his beatings like a man. Richard, he lived alone, a closeted homosexual who bashed in the heads of people he called faggot hippies, all while he did very bad things to many people."

"Jesus, Nick." I looked down at the picture. Just a kid.

"The Russians found that picture in Frank White's bedroom after they killed him. That's what they told me in the woods." Nick pointed to the picture. "Frank kept a file on me. They took pictures of me after my beating. Maybe Frank kept it as some sort of sick trophy, or maybe he was going to use it as a weapon against me if I ever decided to quit working for him. I don't know."

"Why'd Vitali give it to you?"

"So I would never forget." Nick rubbed his tired eyes.

"Christ, man." I didn't know what to say.

"Now you know," Nick told me. "Now you know everything."

Chapter 21

Nick dropped me off in front of our house unceremoniously. We shook hands in the dark of night, and I walked toward the door. That was it. No formal goodbye. He was still in the van, engine idling, as I walked in the house.

I was in shock, to say the least.

Was I really about to skip town? Was I really about to abandon my home, my life? It was unbelievable, unfathomable. Shit like this only happened in the movies. I was never going to see Nick Grady again. That thought hadn't yet sunk in—that I had lost my best friend.

It was better that we didn't say goodbye. It was better to ride off into the sunset ... or moonlight.

Nick's van rumbled down the driveway as I peered through the blinds and watched the taillights disappear. He was off to make the delivery, and I would be gone before the drop was made.

The house was quiet, a thing dead. Without Nick dancing around the place, the house was just an old set of bones decaying in the woods.

I backtracked from the blinds and looked around my room, at my stuff, my belongings. I didn't want any of it. The things in life that I wanted to possess weren't objects that could be packed away in a suitcase. I wanted to hold on to the garden, the music, the target practice by the old stump. Becka's free-spirited nature, her bewildering eyes looking at me in the dead of night. I wanted to keep my youth, Nick's wisdom, and nights spent howling drunk at the moon. I wanted to keep alive the life experiences that had now become nothing more than memories.

I stuffed a few shirts and pants in my duffel bag and pressed them down on top of the wads of wrapped hundred-dollar bills. In the closet, I pulled free the loose edge of the carpet where I kept my stash of money underneath a floorboard. It was everything I had saved up while working for Nick.

It was near midnight when I left the house. Sitting in my car, I looked out the windshield at my house, my home. I tried not to feel nostalgic, but it was difficult knowing that I would never see that old house again.

I started the engine and spun the wheel, going around the circular driveway and out toward the highway. In my rearview mirror, I watched the houselights grow weaker and then disappear.

I spent hours behind the wheel until my eyes were fighting to stay open. I had to stop at the nearest hotel.

My room smelled strongly of mildew, and after a fitful attempt at sleeping on the crummy mattress, I watched the sun begin to rise through the missing slat in the blinds. I tried to let the early morning drift by as I lay in bed. My mind wandered to Becka as I watched whatever crap was on TV, and I fought the urge to look at the phone, her phone number playing over and over in my thoughts.

An hour later, I forced my aching body to stand. I showered, dressed, and walked outside into the bright, blue-skied day.

In the parking lot, I popped the trunk of my old Buick and tossed the duffel bag in the far back. I unlocked the driver's side door—

A dark Cadillac was parked around the bend.

I froze.

"Hello, Mr. Powers," a voice bellowed from my side.

I didn't turn. I didn't move. I couldn't speak. Someone had closed in behind me.

The doors of the Cadillac opened, and the same older, well-dressed Russians stepped out. I didn't know which one was Vitali and which one was Nikolay. The men glanced up at the clear sky, buttoning the top buttons of their suit jackets.

The voice behind me said, "Let's talk."

Still, I didn't move, didn't speak. My heart beat loud in my eardrums and

I felt sweat forming all over my body. My hands turned involuntarily to fists.

The massive bodies of the two young Russians pressed against my back, pushing me forward. A calloused hand pried the room keys out of my fingers, and I walked forward. If this was it, if this was the end, I wasn't going to die sniveling like a whipped dog.

"What do you want?" I asked the voices.

"A little chat. Inside."

They pushed me to the door to my room and put the key in the lock. I was planning on turning fast with a right hook, but a half step in, two massive hands were at the square of my back, shoving me so hard that I fell faster than my legs could keep up. I tripped, hit my chin on the ground, and skittered over the carpet.

"Shit," I let out, before hands were on me again, lifting me high and tossing me effortlessly across the room. I landed hard on my side.

All four men were in the room now, and the door was closed and locked. The curtains were drawn.

"What—what do you want?" I pleaded. "I tried to leave, okay? I know. I tried to skip town. Do you blame me? Do you fucking blame me?"

The hands of that shorter fuck grabbed me, lifting me so quickly that I didn't have time to get away. Then my body reacted. I kicked hard, right between the man's legs.

His stony face contorted, turning crimson, and before he fell to his side I leveled my fist and punched him square on the cheek. My fist felt like it had struck concrete, and pain burst down my forearm. The other three men looked surprised, and the two in the suits chuckled.

"A fiery one we got here, huh?"

Their Russian accents were so slight that they were barely noticeable, washed away by their years in the US.

My arms were cocked to my chest, ready to fight. The other, taller young Russian walked up to me, arms slightly at the ready, a bounce to his step. He bobbed. I swung, and he ducked. I missed, and he bobbed again, landing a fast left jab square into my eye socket. My head jerked back and I saw a dazzling array of blinding-white stars. I didn't see the next punch, but I felt it whack into my nose and then another punch land deep in my stomach. I fell forward, doubling over as blood dripped to the carpet. Then he kicked me onto my side.

"I-I'll come back," I croaked. "I-I shouldn't have left."

Vitali and Nikolay walked over, hovering above me. "This one here," one of them said, patting the tall Russian's shoulder, "he will get the belt one day, no?" He nodded toward the younger man, whom I now presumed was a boxer. Then the boss turned his gaze straight at me. "Where is he?" he demanded.

"W-who? Nick?"

The man whom I had kicked in the balls was regaining his composure, and he stood above me looking angry, and not entirely as short as he had only moments ago. I swallowed. The men in suits nodded to him, and a fist came down heavy on my right side.

I wheezed, the breath taken out of my lungs. Another punch came down, and I thought my ribs were going to shatter. One of them spoke again, "Where is he?"

I choked, trying to inhale as much air as possible. "I-I don't know."

The fist cocked back and I put my hands up, trying to guard my face and body.

"Oh, Christ." I managed a glance in the man's eyes, seeing nothing but crazed anger. Another fist cracked against my ribcage.

"I swear. I swear to you," I pleaded. "I'll tell you whatever you want to know, but I swear to God, I don't know where Nick Grady is. I thought he was making the drop."

The man with the cocked arm relented.

"You think it was smart removing the tracking device from the van?"

"Tracking device? I never saw a tracking device."

"Two days ago the feed went dead, and today the drop is not made. Now, we find you trying to leave town. I told you in the woods, you belong to us. Did you not understand?"

"Where was the tracking device?"

I thought back to two days ago, when we stopped at a hotel for the night.

Nick told me he was leaving to get something to eat, but instead he was calling our landlord, Rob. He must have gone through the cocaine, found the bug and got rid of it.

One of the bosses put his hand inside his jacket. When he brought his hand back out I cowered, ready to feel the cold steel of a gun barrel press against my temple. Instead, something light hit my chest and bounced off. A cheap flip phone fell to the floor.

"You have one day to find him," the man said. "You call the number on speed dial when you do. We will be following that phone, so if it goes dead, you can expect to see our pretty faces again. And we won't be so gentle next time. We will use pipes and sharp blades instead of our fists. We will make you lose every ounce of blood in your body before your life is taken from you. We will show you things, parts of your body hidden by flesh. You will be so happy when it is over and you are allowed to die. So happy. It will go on for days. Do you understand?"

The men were backing toward the door, leaving me on the ground.

"I-I understand." I looked at the phone. I didn't know if I could do this— try to find Nick so that these guys could kill him.

"You have one day. Twenty-four hours."

"Yes—yes, Vitali."

The man paused.

"No," the man said, looking at his partner. "I am not Vitali."

I really didn't care who was who.

"Here," the other man said. He reached inside his coat pocket. "When you find Nick, you can give him this." He produced a Polaroid picture, and let it flutter to my face. I took it from the ground and grimaced, expecting to see another bloody picture of a young Nick Grady.

But it was not Nick in the picture.

"You … motherfuckers. You fucking—"

I moved to stand, my heart beating my vision red. The short fucker whom I had the pleasure of kicking in the balls struck me back down with a heel to the chest.

The picture fell from my hands.

"Oh," the older Russian said, "I see you have a fondness for the girl, no?" He laughed.

I looked at the picture of Becka sitting before a wooden table with a rag tied over her eyes, a gag in her mouth. Her wrists were bound, but resting on the tabletop. A large man stood behind her wearing a black ski mask, his disgusting palm gripping her shoulder, befouling the silver chain of the locket I had given her.

"If you so much as—"

"You have twenty-four hours, Mr. Powers."

"I'll—"

"Twenty-four hours, or we will kill this girl you are so fond of."

The fist came back and walloped my eye socket, displaying a brilliant array of silver and red stars like fireworks. The men were gone before my eyesight returned.

Chapter 22

The car engine idled, but I didn't know where to go.

What the fuck …

My swollen eye and battered nose looked awful in the rearview mirror. I'd taken worse beatings, but goddamn those big guys sure knew how to throw a punch.

I had to find Nick, that was certain. I wasn't sure what I would do when I found him, but one thing was absolute: I wasn't simply going to turn him over to the Russians. They would kill him, most likely. Torture him for days. I had to believe that Nick could get us out of this mess. Maybe there was still some hope. I had to believe that there *was* still hope, because if there wasn't, the alternatives were terrifying.

Becka …

The Russians were trying to get me all riled up to hunt Nick down, and it was working.

I thought about my conversation with Nick in the van just a few days ago.

"The best thing to do is leave her alone. Don't contact her," he had said.

He had been adamant about not talking to her, trying to protect her. And now, these Russian scumbags had her tied up, tortured. Jesus, she must be terrified. I envisioned her in some dark corner, a sour-smelling bag over her beautiful face. Her fear must be awful.

I had to find Nick.

The problem was, I had no idea where to begin. My first logical thought was to check back at home, but the Russians had surely looked for him there.

I couldn't think of a single person other than Darin, Becka, and myself who might know where Nick would hide.

And then it hit me—there *was* one other person whom Nick confided in. One other person who might know where to find him: Jim Hoffman. It was worth a shot. He was Nick's oldest friend, practically his partner. Jim had even worked with the Russians back in the '60s, growing pot out of their little storage shed.

Nick told me that Jim had skipped town, but I never fully believed him. The guy hadn't skipped town back when Nick first got involved with the Russians, and he even stuck around when Nick got pulled into Frank White's operation. Besides, the Russians weren't looking for him. The guy was a botanist. He had nothing to do with distribution or sales. If anything, Jim was probably hiding out locally—and I knew just where to start looking.

I put the car in reverse, backed out of the parking lot, and turned onto the freeway. It took me about two hours until I was back in my neighborhood, and I drove on, deeper into the Barrens. First, I passed Jim's house, just to make sure that he wasn't home. When I passed his little bungalow in the woods, I didn't see his familiar white sedan parked out front. The house was dark and quiet.

I parked and got out anyway, walking in a wide swoop across his property, trying to look in his windows as I approached. But there was nothing to see; the curtains were all drawn. I knocked several times on his door, but to no avail. After a moment, I tried the handle, but as expected, it was locked. If he was home, he had barricaded himself inside, and I wasn't about to start kicking the door down. Not yet, anyway. I had another idea.

Back in my car, I drove on, going east, further away from the sandy soil of the Barrens and toward the flat farms and gardens outside of the woods. A few miles passed, and then I saw the field of gold.

The worm farm.

From the road, the dilapidated service barn stood out in the distance. I turned slowly onto the dirt driveway and approached. Cheryl's pickup truck was parked to the side.

She heard my car crunching down on the gravel as I neared, and soon she came out from the barn, putting down a crate of something that looked heavy. She wiped her brow with one hand, using the other to shield her eyes from the sun. I parked only feet from where she stood.

I opened the door.

"Cheryl," I said, getting out.

"Powers, man. What are you doing here?"

Her expression looked fierce, but it might have been the sun glaring into her eyes.

I wasn't exactly sure how to play this out, so I stayed cool.

"Hey," I said. "You seen Jim around?"

She shook her head, her massive dreadlocks swaying, seeming to pull her head back. "No man, haven't heard from him since last I saw you. Why? What's up?"

I shrugged, trying my best to appear calm. "I've been looking for him, but he's not home. You haven't talked to him at all in the last few days? You don't know where he is?"

"No man. What's this about?"

"What about Nick? He been around?"

"Thought he was with you."

"Who told you that?"

She shrugged. "You're roommates, right?"

"Right. Of course."

"He missing or something?"

"Who, Jim?"

"Both of them, I guess, if you're asking around."

"Nah, nothing like that."

We were silent for a moment. I let the silence continue, creep into her thoughts. Play tricks on her mind.

"Wanna smoke a joint or something?" She swallowed. Her voice had a quiver.

I looked right in her eyes.

"What's up with you and Becka? You have a fight or something back in the day?"

"No man, nothing like that. I was just stoned that day, man. I didn't mean nothing by it. You come all this way to ask about Becka?"

I shook my head. "No. Looking for Jim, remember? It's important."

"Is—is everything all right? Is he in danger?"

I shrugged. "Nah, I'm sure he'll be fine. Some people speaking in accents came looking for him. Not sure why. It's probably nothing."

"The Russians are looking for him? What did they say?"

"Yeah, I guess they sounded Russian. They didn't say much, just that they want to talk to him. Everyone just up and vanished."

"Is he in danger?"

I shrugged. "All they asked was if I knew where he's been. I said to check his house. Then I thought about you, and I started thinking, well, maybe Cheryl can help them out."

"You told them about me? Powers, *what* exactly did they say? What do they want?"

I stared right in her squinting eyes. Her hand shielding the sun seemed to be trembling.

"Hey, I gotta split. You see Jim, tell him I came looking. All right?"

"Powers?"

"See ya, Cheryl."

I went back to the car. Cheryl followed me to the door.

"Powers, tell me what they want."

"Sorry, don't know."

I swung the car around and got out of there, watching her in the rearview mirror, her hand still shielding her eyes.

The good thing about the worm farm was that it was isolated. At least the service entrance was. From the driveway, the single road led to highways on either end, miles in between. I drove up the driveway, and then I took a gamble. Taking a right would lead me further east, out of the Barrens and out of New Jersey. Taking a left led back into the woods, the way I had come.

I took a left and drove to the first major intersection, about five miles up the road. There was an old biker bar on the corner that sold two types of bottled beer and several-day-old deviled eggs. There were never more than a few trucks and bikes parked out front, and maybe a person or two smoking outside. I pulled in and parked around the rear of the building, blocking the view of my car from oncoming traffic.

A minute passed, and I was starting to have doubts.

But this was do-or-die time, and I wasn't about to start dying. Moving fast, I grabbed the two tracking devices from the passenger seat and walked quickly to the side of the building where three Harleys sat idle. One tracking device was the cell phone, and the other was a little black box, about the size of two cigarette packs, with a stubby antenna sticking out from the side. That device I had found secured under my car by a magnet that was practically strong enough to weld itself to the metal. I was exposed out there by the bikes, but I didn't see a soul around. Nobody smoking out front, and no cars driving down the highway. My hands trembled with adrenaline as I went to the first bike and tried the saddle. It was a metal box on the back of the bike, and it was locked. I tried the next bike, pulling on the door to the compartment, and my heart skipped a beat as the lid opened. I pushed the two devices under a pair of gloves and some other article of clothing, and turned, practically running back to the car.

I stared at the bike, my heart pounding, expecting a gang of bikers to come running out thinking I put a bomb or something in their bikes. But no one came out. I knew most of the bike gangs in these parts anyway, having dealt with the Barren Souls back when I tended bar. I could probably have talked myself out of a confrontation if necessary, thrown a few names around.

Sitting there, catching my breath, I focused again on the quiet road. Time seemed to be flying away like dry leaves in the wind, but in reality only minutes passed.

Then, all at once, it happened.

Cheryl's truck passed so fast that I barely heard it coming.

Hook, line, and sinker.

I started the ignition, turned the wheel, and sped out onto the highway.

Chapter 23

Cheryl's pickup cut through the quiet roads. I stayed behind, nearly out of sight. I got worried each time she went over a hill or turned out of view that I would lose her completely.

We drove back the way I had come, and I thought I knew for sure where she was going, and I felt stupid for not investigating further when I had the chance. But then I saw her pass Jim's house and continue over the winding road.

I was constantly on the lookout for other cars, particularly a dark Cadillac, my eyes darting between the rearview and side mirrors. But there was nothing to suggest that Vitali and Nikolay had eyes on me. The roads were quiet, nearly deserted.

Past a bend far up the road, I saw the red of Cheryl's brake lights as she took a slow right-hand turn and then came to a stop. I quickly pulled over, hoping that she hadn't seen me. Then she continued driving, disappearing behind a thicket on the side of the road.

After a moment, I put the car back in drive and passed the driveway Cheryl had turned into. A tall chain-link fence with a security keypad guarded the entrance. The fence went on for what looked like miles in both directions, and it was covered in thick vines and bramble that made it almost invisible.

I had a good idea where I was—Jim's summer home.

I passed the entrance and parked the car on the other side of the road, got out, and looked around. The air was still and quiet. A portion of the chain-link fence near the entrance was clear of vines and brush, yet far enough away from the security camera mounted over the keypad. I grabbed hold of the crisscrossing metal and began pulling myself up. Halfway over the other side, I jumped to the bottom. For a moment, I took in my surroundings: woods in all direction and a dirt driveway snaking away from the gate. What caught my attention was a tree directly across from me with a small rectangular device mounted near the bottom. A round lens with a sheer side stared at me. I knew what I was looking at: a motion sensor with night vision optics. We used the same ones in the warehouse. If Jim were indeed behind those gates, he would now be alerted to my presence.

Since there was no use shielding myself anymore, I walked fast to the dirt driveway, and then began running along the twisting path. In the near distance, a cabin came into view.

Then I saw some reassurance parked next to Cheryl's truck: Jim's white sedan. A moment later, I saw Jim himself, rushing toward me with his back hugging the brush on the side of the road. He had a crazed look that was made all the more wild by his scraggly beard. The .12 gauge shotgun pressed against his hairy chest helped too.

"Hey, Jim. Jim!" I called out, waving my hands before me.

Jim stopped and raised the gun, squinting in my direction.

"Powers? Is that you?"

"Jim, man. It's so good to see you, you have no idea."

Jim shook his head. "You shouldn't be here."

"Yeah, I keep hearing that. I need your help."

We met in the driveway, his shotgun lowered. Jim looked like he hadn't washed in a week.

"What's going on?" he asked.

"It's Nick. Have you seen him?"

Jim didn't answer.

"It's—we're in trouble, man. We're in trouble. I need your help."

"Cheryl just got here, saying something about you accosting her at the farm? What's this about the Russians looking for me? Powers, tell me what's going on." He didn't look happy. "Now."

I shook my head fervently. "They're not looking for you. I'm sorry, man, but it was the only way I could find you. What is this place? This the summer home I always hear about?"

Jim didn't answer. He pushed his glasses up his nose and scratched the side of his beard. "All right, let's talk. Let's go to the house."

We walked slowly up the driveway, and I started blabbering. I told him everything that had happened over the last several days. The words just flew out of my mouth. The ride to British Columbia, the Russians, the cocaine. By the time we reached the cabin, with the long and narrow greenhouse attached to its side, Jim stopped in his tracks.

"Wait? The Russians, they tracked you?"

"They placed a bug under my car—"

"And you're here? *Powers!*"

It was strange seeing this man whom I had only ever known as being a cheerful, almost cartoonish hippie, suddenly so ferocious.

"It's cool, man. It's cool. I left the tracking device behind, far away. They don't know where I am."

Jim stared toward the greenhouse attached to the cabin where he grew his private field of marijuana. These were Jim's legendary crops. These were his beloved mother plants—the plants used to fuel the operation. His prized and coveted babies. He only ever brought in cuttings from these plants, dipped in a rooting hormone, and stuck in root plugs until they established growth. Nick had told me that some of his mother plants could be traced back to the original, all those years ago when they had first started growing.

"Hey," I said. "Can we go inside?"

Jim began walking briskly toward his cabin and yelled behind him, "No, Powers. Leave—now."

I walked after him. "Jim?"

He swung around, shotgun aimed squarely at my torso.

"Powers—fuck off! You have no idea what you're messed up in. Get the hell out of here. Now! I'm not fucking around!" He pumped the shotgun purely for effect. The shell that had already been loaded in the chamber spiraled to the ground and bounced off into the grass.

I stopped short, hands up. Jim looked wild. No longer that careless free spirit, but a true psychopath in the woods.

"Listen. They have Becka, Jim. The Russians have her, and God knows what they're doing to her."

Jim stared straight at me, and said, "How do you know this?"

"They showed me a picture. It's in my pocket if you don't believe me. She was tied up. Jim, you gotta tell me where Nick is."

Jim didn't speak, didn't move.

"Jim?"

He shook his head. "Can't believe a word those guys tell you. Everything they say is a lie. Powers, get the fuck off of my property. I'm not going to tell you again."

"All right, all right. Okay. I'm leaving, Jim. I'm leaving. Just tell me— *where* is he? Where is Nick?"

"Nick?" he laughed. Actually laughed. "Nick's done running, man."

"What's that supposed to mean?"

"The guy is through. Quits."

"Was he here?"

Jim shook his head. "It doesn't matter."

"Tell me, Jim. I'm going, I'll leave right now. I'm not fucking around." I looked straight in his eyes, narrowing my gaze. "One of us has to be a fucking man and help Becka. You can stay here with that bitch Cheryl, and weather things out like you always do."

He didn't have the balls to pull the trigger. We both knew this.

"Use your head, man," he said. "Yeah, Nick was here. Listen, danger follows that man like the plague. Take my advice: if you can lose the Russians you should run far, far away. Let Nick deal with saving Becka. Get the hell out of here. You're still young."

I shook my head. "Where'd he go, Jim? Just tell me where he went."

Jim rested his shotgun against his shoulder.

"He left about a half hour ago. Told me he was done running. Where do you think he's heading?"

I shrugged.

"Home," he said. "He's going home."

"The Russians will be checking the house, probably have someone staked out there."

"He knows that."

It took a moment for me to process that Nick had indeed given up. He was going home to make a final stand. Maybe if I could get there before the Russians I could persuade him to change his mind. If Nick was truly giving up, if Nick were to die, there would be nobody left to help me save Becka, help me break free from the grip the Russians would have on me for the rest of my life. I could be tortured for his actions.

"Now, will you kindly get the fuck off my property?"

I turned and ran back the way I'd come.

Chapter 24

I parked on the side of the road and sat watching the house.

He was there.

His van was visible through the brush.

I was paralyzed.

What was I going to do?

What was I going to say?

I heard a familiar sound nearby—a cracking noise that I knew all too well.

After a long breath, I started the car and I pulled into the driveway.

Nick's van was parked close to the front door, the lettering of Grady Construction and Repair in desperate need of a fresh coat of paint. I parked beside it.

And there he was, out by the garden. Just like old times. But unlike old times, his CD player was not with him, blaring the Dead. He saw me, but he didn't turn around as I approached. Garden equipment sat piled in a heap. The bow rake, with its row of sharp metal teeth, leaned against one of the Adirondack chairs. The soil had been turned over, just as he had told our landlord he would do. Perhaps he had not given up. Not entirely.

But instead of laying the grass seed down, Nick was refilling his black powder pistol.

When I got within earshot he spoke.

"Hello, Powers."

"Hello, Nick."

I eyed an unopened bottle of Jack on the arm of the Adirondack chair. On the other arm was Nick's second black powder pistol. I picked it up out of habit and began filling each chamber with powder.

I asked him, "When did you dump the coke?"

"Same night I called Rob. You shouldn't be here, you know."

"I know."

With our pistols armed, we walked a few steps into the yard. We weren't practicing our quick draw, but rather aimed our pistols at the cans set up on the stump and fired deliberate shots.

He asked, "What happened to your face?"

"You know what happened."

He didn't reply.

We fired another round.

"This is over." I tightened my grip on the pistol. "The Russians, they're looking for you. They have Becka."

There was a pause. I eyed him out of the corner of my vision, saw his revolver waver.

"They're threatening to kill her if you don't turn yourself in."

"How—did they tell you this? Where do they have her?"

I fished in my pocket, showing Nick the picture they'd given me. He glanced at it, then looked away, disgusted.

"Oh, Jesus Christ."

"We have to go get her," I said.

"Powers, man." He shook his head. Then he leveled his pistol at the targets. "No. We won't save her by confronting the Russians head-on. How did this happen?" He looked sharply at me. "You didn't talk to her, did you?"

"No, Nick. I said that I wouldn't, and I keep my word."

He grilled me a moment longer, then turned back toward the targets.

"I'll wait for them here. Let them come get me. I'll make a call, get a shotgun and an assault rifle. You get the hell out of here, Powers. Let me deal with this."

"You know I can't do that."

"Powers—"

"I'm not going anywhere. We're in this together, Nick."

He seemed to think this over, and then he sighed. "All right, man. All right."

"Why aren't the Russians watching the place?" I scanned the quiet property. The only noise, other than our bullet fire, was the trees in the wind.

Nick didn't say anything.

After a moment of contemplation, Nick spoke. "Okay, Powers, if we're in this together, I'm going to lay some stuff on you, so don't ..." His words cut short, his throat constricting.

"How the fuck do I know if I can trust you anymore?"

He swallowed. "Maybe you can't. That's for you to decide. I'm done running. I'm done lying. Just hear me out. It's time I told you the truth. It's not fair to you anymore, and I'd rather you hear it from me now than the Russians later. Just remember, I was only trying to protect you this entire time." He looked toward the stump, the two of us side by side, looking away from each other's eyes.

"Back in the sixties, Frank White had been working with Vitali and Nikolay for months before the shoot-out in the warehouse. They were going to make some serious changes to the operation. Vitali and Nikolay were young and idealistic. Belonging to the ancient Russian regime wasn't who they were. Being in America during that time changed them on an almost spiritual level. Drugs were rampant—acid, mushrooms. I know I made them out to be real slick types, but to be honest, they were just kids who didn't know what to do with the power that they possessed. What they were planning was to break their ties with the Russian organization and branch out on their own. Frank White offered them a way to get rid of their crew, send their men back to their motherland. Most of the operation then, Vitali and Nikolay included, were illegal immigrants. Exporting them out of the country or sending them to jail wouldn't have been difficult."

Nick paused, aimed his pistol, and fired.

The boom echoed loud. The smell of gunpowder drifted in the air. I followed suit, not really aiming. We fired until our chambers were empty, then Nick walked off toward the Adirondack chairs and began cleaning and rearming the cylinder.

He continued. "That day at the warehouse, the shoot-out, it was never supposed to happen. Vitali and Nikolay, they were planning to continue working with my partners and myself once the separation went down. Their organization wouldn't simply let them walk away; once you were a member of their crew, you were theirs for life. Things were in the works, like new identities, new appearances. Frank had worked on setting things up for them—for a price, of course. But I found out too late that he was only looking out for himself, Richard, and Martin. But then that fateful day, Frank gets shot before their plan could go into effect, and he scrambled out of there, nearly bleeding to death against the side of the van. Then out runs young Nick Grady."

We both looked up. There was a noise in the distance, not far. After a moment, the car turned onto the driveway.

"Nick." My voice wavered. "I don't think you have time to get that shotgun."

The black Cadillac parked.

Chapter 25

Nick swatted the box of pistol balls and powder to the grass, and tucked his half-armed pistol in the back of his shorts.

"Get it out of sight," he hissed at me.

I tucked my pistol in the rear of my jeans.

"You shouldn't be here," he repeated.

"Jesus Christ, I know that already." I swallowed. "These guys, they're not going to be fucking around."

"No shit."

The car parked and the driver and passenger got out. They opened the back doors, and the bosses appeared, crisping the collars of their shirts and buttoning their coats. They saw us clear as day, yet looked up at the sky as if enjoying the feeling of the sun on their faces.

My eyes twitched to the sealed bottle of whiskey. My mouth felt impossibly dry. Licking my lips only seemed to suck away any remaining moisture.

My voice croaked, "What happened next?"

"Frank White pulled the trigger."

I swallowed.

"Vitali and Nikolay came bursting out of the warehouse, and when they saw Frank had been shot, the badge in his hand, the body of a teenage boy by his side, they quickly ran back to the warehouse door and stopped the rest of their men from rushing outside. They ordered their crew to lock the doors, barricade the warehouse. They dragged Frank inside the van and dumped Nick Grady in the trunk."

I cleared my raw throat. "You're ..."

"My name is Nick Grady. I *am* Nick Grady. I have become Nick Grady." He turned to me. "Do you understand?"

I nodded.

"They took me and Nikolay to the station and beat us senseless. That much is true."

"That picture you showed me."

Nick nodded. "That was after the plastic surgery. I took his identity. I am Nick Grady. It was the perfect move. But I was too young and naive to know that Frank and his men were going to abuse us for the rest of our lives. Everything changed when we moved to America. We were swept up in the craziness of the times. All we wanted to do was sell pot and join in on the party. Hardcore organized crime wasn't for us. We wanted to be revolutionary in our business, lead our organization through positive motivation, we had so many ideals back then. We thought we were doing good, selling pot to hippies. After my plastic surgery healed, the ruse worked. The Russians never suspected that Nikolay and I had changed our identities. The police made it appear that we escaped back to Russia, and they've been looking for us there ever since. But that all changed when they murdered Frank White and found his stash: pictures, medical reports ... everything he'd saved to blackmail me if ever needed." Nick shook his head.

"Your voice, though."

"Losing my accent was the easiest part of becoming Nick Grady."

"What happened to Nikolay?"

"My brother? I believe you just saw him."

"Jim?"

Nick nodded.

"Frank and his men killed Jim Hoffman in his grow room and got rid of his body. Nick and Jim, they were only a few years younger than us, making the transformation that much easier. Nick's small operation was wiped out in a day, and we took it over."

I nodded toward the Russians, who were halfway across the yard. "So these guys?"

"Are very angry with me."

"Who are they?"

"They took over the operation when Nikolay and I escaped, some up-and-comers sent in from Russia. Twins. They've been using our names, our identities—Nikolay and I—to keep what business they could after we disappeared. It doesn't matter who they are."

"Where does Becka fit in with all of this?"

Nick sighed and shrugged. "Same as you. She was some hippie girl who always showed up at parties. She was eighteen when I met her. No family, nothing. Just a drifter. She sure as shit would have died on the streets. She was filthy, just a kid following bands around and no one to watch over her. I gave her some cash and a bed to crash on once in a while. The girl was already swinging dope at all the shows, so I set her up with some of my product—better product than she was selling. After a few years, I set her up in the warehouse so she could settle down, work a solid job."

The Russians were now within earshot. Nick stopped talking, staring straight at them through crazed eyes.

"Hello, Nick," one of the twins bellowed. "Or does he not yet know?" The man nodded toward me.

"Where is she?" Nick, or Vitali, said in a growl.

The men stopped and stared at us. The two lieutenants, the big goons, stood with their hands clasped at their belt buckles, only inches from their pistols hidden behind open jackets. The man whom I had kicked in the balls stood straight across from me, holding a duffel bag. He stared right into my eyes, cracking a cruel and amused smile.

"Vitali, Vitali, Vitali … what am I going to do with you?" The one twin shook his head. "So many chances we give you, and still, you fuck us over."

"My name is Nick Grady. Let the boy go."

"Where's Marcus?" The twin looked around the yard.

Nick shrugged. "Let the boy go. This is between us."

All eyes flickered to me. "Too late for that, I'm afraid. Wrong place, wrong time. Does the boy know everything? Does he know what happened to you in that basement, all those years ago?" The man smirked.

Nick opened his mouth to speak, but nothing came out.

I was about to say that I knew everything. Nick had told me about the beating.

But the man continued, "Does he know what they did to you on that table? That they bent you over and held you down? Hmm?"

The other twin continued, "Does he know about the cop, Richard, coming back to your house many times, making sure that you understood who was in charge? Does he know that they kept pictures? Pictures of you being abused, sodomized."

"And I killed that son of a bitch!" Nick hissed, the word trailing spittle from his lips. His body tensed, and so did mine. "I ended it one day when that piece of shit came over unannounced. I hid around the corner of the bathroom's second doorway, with the shower water running. That asshole came right in, walking quietly toward the bathroom undoing his belt, thinking he would take me by surprise. He had another think coming. When Richard pulled the curtain back I came around the corner and shot that piece of shit right in the back of his head." Nick pointed to the base of his own head with two fingers, making a shooting motion. His eyes were huge. "The bullet from my .22 stayed in his skull, and I pushed him into the water to bleed out. His arms flapped around, beat at the water. Nobody knew that I killed him. Not Frank—nobody. Dozens of people wanted that asshole dead. I left him in the woods to rot. I left him for the wolves and the worms. I did the world a favor."

My legs felt like they were going to give out. I could hear in my head the many times Nick had drunkenly screamed out, *"I-I was a just a k-kid ..."*

Everyone was silent, and then one of the bosses shooed his hands dismissively.

"Whatever the case," he said. "You have not accepted our offer for redemption, to come back to our organization. *Your* organization."

Nick didn't speak. I could hear his heavy breathing.

"I suppose this day was inevitable." The man sighed. "I have something here for you." He nodded to his lieutenant, and the man reached into the duffel bag, producing something dark and slack in his fingers. He tossed it to the ground before our feet. Nick and I recoiled. My heart drummed, thinking that it was Becka's dark hair we were seeing, stained red. But it was not. The hair was too black and straight. It belonged to Darin. The man reached in again and tossed another slack object to the grass, followed by a pair of shattered glasses.

"My brother," Nick muttered.

The man looked straight into Nick's eyes. "You are responsible for the death of your loved ones, Vitali. Everyone around you dies. You are a plague onto the world."

There was no time to process what happened next until it was over. The events transpired in mere seconds. Just a blur. Yet each frame became burned in my mind.

The goons budged a half step toward us, their hands moving into their jackets.

Nick's eyes twitched, and the bosses had a split second to react before Nick reached behind his back and swung out before him his large revolver in one fluid and practiced motion. The hammer was already cocked, and when he pulled the trigger a thunderclap filled the air. The head of the tall lieutenant snapped violently backwards, and the man fell hard to the ground. The gun was then focused at the boss beside the lieutenant and the trigger was pulled. At the same time, the other boss and lieutenant jerked to their sides, pulling out their guns. Nick fired a third shot at the remaining boss, a burst of smoke and sparks billowing from the pistol barrel. The round struck the man square in the chest. The twin doubled over and fell backward.

The stocky man before me had unholstered his pistol. My body moved faster than my mind could register as I grabbed the handle of the black powder pistol and swung it at the bastard's chest. When I pulled the trigger the gun bucked like it had never bucked before, and the handle flew out of my grip. Before these men arrived, I hadn't had time to seal the chambers with grease. Three of the bullets erupted in a chain fire, pelting the man's abdomen and shoulder. The man stammered, squeezing off rounds as his hand clamped up. But he didn't fall. I grabbed the sleek wooden handle of the gardening rake from where it rested against the Adirondack chair, and I swung it at the man's chest like a baseball bat. The man shrieked and toppled onto his back, the metal stakes of the rake planted in his ribcage. His hands twitched over the handle, flapping like fish out of water, and he made an awful fluid-filled gurgle. Then his body went slack. I looked down at the four men on the ground, the soil thirsting for their blood.

They did not move.

"H-Holy shit, Nick. Nick?"

I turned, the blood pumping so fast in my veins that my vision flashed red and white.

"Nick!"

Nick Grady lay in the grass behind me, his clear blue eyes staring up at the limitless sky. A bullet had struck him square in the jaw under his lower teeth. His face was unrecognizable. His hands convulsed at his sides and he made an awful sound that will haunt me until my last day on earth.

I stayed kneeling by his side until Nick stopped moving, and his eyes glazed, stared up to the heavens.

"Nick ... oh man, oh no. Come on, Nick." I shook his shoulders, but it was pointless.

There was a faint noise behind me. The sound of a dying man dragging himself across the lawn.

I stood and turned to see one of the twins inching away, pulling at the grass in desperate handfuls. Looking among the gardening tools, I found the spade shovel with the heavy wooden handle and sharpened edge. I grabbed the dying man by the back of his shoulder, and flung him around to face me.

He made a sound like, "Ahhgg, fu-fu-fu-fuck." He was bleeding up pools.

The weight of the shovel felt good in my hands. The sleek wood felt nice, cool and smooth.

I glared down at him.

Chapter 26

Comprehending everything that had just happened would take a while. My heart was racing, yet my mind felt still. Focused.

Becka still had to be saved.

And I had a plan.

So I started working fast, trying not to dwell on what had just happened—what was still happening. That would be for later, when the crushing pains of reality could be properly dealt with.

Nick had pre-dug a large pit in the back of the garden where the soil was soft. It startled me to find a corpse already lying facedown in the dirt when I pulled the bodies of the dead Russians to the edge and pushed them over with my heel. I could only guess that the body belonged to Marcus, the guy the twin had mentioned. And I could only guess that Marcus had been watching the house when Nick arrived.

All I had were guesses.

I took one last look at the bodies of the Russians lying together in a jumbled heap and shoveled soil over their tangled corpses.

Under the shade of the apple tree was where I dug Nick's grave, deep and alone.

That Russian fucker lost blood too quickly for me to get much out of him. But I got a few words. In the end, the guy actually laughed—*laughed*—when I stood over him, shovel in hand, demanding to know where Becka was being held.

"You-you-you fool!" he said, laughing. Dying.

But he did tell me where Becka was. Sputtering up blood in fluid-filled coughs, he told me.

"Sh-she's right under your nose. You'll never get her out of the warehouse," he said through ragged breaths. "She-she-she's not going anywhere, that bitch. They have orders to k-kill her if anything g-goes wrong."

When his coughing turned worse, the blood foaming at his lips, I stood and watched as his life drifted away. I made no effort to turn him over and let the fluid drain from his lungs, keeping him alive a little longer.

I was happy to see him dead.

Oh, and I had a few ideas on how to get Becka out of the warehouse. I had a few ideas on how to bury *all* of those Russian scumbags once and for all. Burn them to the ground for what they'd done. Not only to Becka, but to Nick, to myself. Whatever, whoever Nick Grady had been, I had only known him as a friend, and I would never have known his dark secrets if it weren't for these power-hungry assholes. Life would have gone on uninterrupted, and instead of burying my friend under the shade of the apple tree, I would have been drinking a beer, watching him dance to his music as the sprinkler made the vegetables glimmer under the evening sun.

I tried not to think such happy thoughts. It was time to set my plan in motion.

And all it took was two phone calls.

I was quick to bury the dead, and I washed my face and arms with hose water before hightailing it to my Buick, and out onto the road. I was at the office in record time, noticing how much of the gore still covered my body, face and hair. The hose water did little to nothing.

At some point, the office had been cleared out. The desk was ransacked and the filing cabinets wiped clean. By whom, I didn't know. Perhaps Jim had cleared it out while we were making the delivery, but most likely it was the Russians. I say that because the ledgers remained under the false molding, and the safe was still intact behind the wainscoting. The office had been raided hastily, and all the important stuff had been missed. I took what I needed, sealed everything back up, and sped back home.

I got out of the car and waited, chain-smoking cigarettes and listening to the wind for any signs of disturbance. That's the thing with bikers; they're not so good at making a quiet entrance.

The minutes ticked by as if trampling through mud. But still, it didn't take long until I heard rumbling in the distance, quiet at first, then steadily growing louder.

Then their bikes thundered into the driveway, three of them, pulling around to meet me where I stood leaning against my car.

They parked, killed their engines, and heeled down their kickstands. Dale Erickson stared right at me, his sickening gaze scanning me over. The vice president, a fat fuck with a great red beard they called Roth, stood by Dale's side. The other guy I didn't recognize, but his insignia indicated he was the sergeant-of-arms. Faded tattoos poked out from his shirt collar, traveling up his neck, nearly to his bald head. When he opened his mouth, a few teeth were missing.

I met them in the driveway, bottle of bourbon in hand, my body filthy.

"Powers," Dale said, squinting against the sun. "So Barry gave you my number, huh? I didn't think I'd ever see you again, with you leaving the brotherhood just days before your inauguration. You're lucky to still be alive. So what's so important that you can't tell me over the phone? You look like hell, by the way."

"Same to you." Barry's was the first number I'd called, offering my old boss, the owner of Whiskey Sins, five hundred dollars for Dale's number. "What I got to talk to you about is business."

"Yeah? And what kind of business you need from me?"

"A few things."

"Hope you got some money, 'cause we don't come cheap."

"I got money, if that's what you want. But the real question you should be asking yourself is *not* what business I need from you, but what business you'll get from me. I can pay you … or I can offer a much more lucrative offer. Income for years—a lifetime."

He nodded. Roth and the sergeant-of-arms stared at me, arms crossed.

"I'm here because you're a good egg, Powers. You were a stand-up bartender, and Barry always talked highly of you. But that's about all you're worth to me, and it ain't much. So start talking."

Dale leaned against his bike, dirty boots crossed at the ankle, fingers clasped at his belt. The garish tattoos covering his hands, fingers, and arms were faded to near obscurity. He spat to the side.

"As of today," I began, "just hours ago, I became the sole proprietor of a fully functioning marijuana growing facility."

"Good for you."

"Nick Grady's operation."

He was silent. The Barren Souls sold everything from cigarettes to methamphetamine, but Nick Grady had been the key weed supplier in the area for decades.

"How would you like a piece?"

"And you're just going to give it to me? A piece of Nick Grady's operation?"

His vice president chimed in. "What's the catch?"

"You're going to help me save a girl," I explained. "And secure the warehouse where the business is located. The operation has been taken over by several armed Russian businessmen, four of whom have already been eliminated. Inside the warehouse, a girl is being held hostage. The deal is this: we take back the warehouse—now, tonight—and eliminate the opposition. Afterwards, I will hand you Nick's network. It can all be yours. The plants are growing as we speak. The four men who have already been eliminated were high up, so if we move quickly we might catch them off guard."

Dale looked me over, and then glanced around the property, to the Cadillac and Nick's van parked in the driveway.

"What exactly happened here?"

I didn't say anything.

"All right," he said. "You got me listening. Give me some numbers."

"Come with me." I nodded toward the Adirondack chairs, and began walking. They followed, and once there, I displayed the ringed binder I'd taken from the safe.

"This is the last five years of sales and profit. End of the year numbers."

Dale scratched the side of his bristled cheek, flipping from page to page.

"You planning on remaining boss of this operation after shit goes down?"

I shrugged. "Maybe. Might need me around, overseeing production, and I might want to be there."

"How do I know you'll keep your word?"

I picked up the bottle of bourbon and unscrewed the top, snapping the plastic seal off the cap.

"'Cause if I'm lying, you'll kill me."

I took a swig, feeling the firewater fill my stomach with heat. I offered the bottle to Dale.

"Damn straight." He took the bottle and drank, passing it back to Roth and his sergeant-of-arms. "How many men we up against?"

"I don't know. Maybe five, maybe more."

"You got a layout of this place? A way in?"

"Know it by heart. I have a master code for the security lock, but if it doesn't work, we'll have to be creative."

Dale nodded and pulled a pack of cigarettes from his pocket, then flicked a battered Zippo open with his free hand.

"Roth, what you thinking?"

The vice president spoke in a gruff voice. "Nick Grady's operation is well known, the thing of legends. Been running since before I was born. Sounds clear-cut to me."

"Jones, what about you?"

"I say we move."

"All right then."

Dale looked over the numbers from the folder for a moment longer, then closed the book. He reached in his pocket and dug out a cell phone.

He dialed and then spoke. "Round 'em up. Twenty men .... Vans, we're going in quiet and heavy. That's right ... bring a battering ram."

He gave whoever he was talking to my address and then hung up.

"We got an hour until they're assembled, so start drawing out the floor plan."

"One other thing." I looked straight in his eyes. "Until this shit's over, I'm the boss. You take orders from me. I'm first in that building, and if a hair on the girl's head is hurt, I want the balls of the man responsible."

Dale smirked. "Powers, I never knew you had it in you." His eyes darted again to my filthy shirt and blood-speckled arms and face. "What the fuck happened here?"

"And I need that Cadillac and the van in the driveway gone. Get rid of them. Make them disappear, chop 'em for parts—I don't care. And I got a few pistols that need to be melted down." I pointed to the black powder pistols on the grass, and the guns from the Russians.

Dale chuckled. "You got it, boss."

***

The men arrived, looking like more of a gang of derelicts in well-worn leather jackets rather than an organized group of professionals.

Fucking bikers.

But at least they looked tough, well-focused. Like they'd done this sort of thing a million times before … a normal day for this band of degenerates.

Three vans pulled up and the men poured out. They had an arsenal of assault rifles and shotguns. I was offered a rifle, but declined, choosing an automatic pistol and a few spare magazines instead. I also took one of the bulletproof vests that the guys were all strapping under their leather jackets, getting themselves ready for war.

As the men piled into the vans, they were given their orders and told what to do once the door was down. The Cadillac and Nick's work van were driven out of sight.

I drove my own Buick with Dale in the passenger seat, Roth and the sergeant-of-arms in the back.

Before we left, Dale asked me, "You want to clean up a bit?"

"Nah," I said. "This is the face I want them to see."

"You crazier than a shit-bird, you know that?" He laughed. "I'm starting to like you, Powers. Might just give you another opportunity to join the brotherhood after this whole clusterfuck goes down."

"We'll see."

We drove the speed limit on those twisting roads until we arrived at the industrial section. I parked at the end of the parking lot, far from the warehouse, and the vans came to a halt. The men jumped out, and we approached on foot. The evening had grown dark.

The warehouse looked quiet, a thing dead. I took lead, the line of men trailing behind me. We hugged the side of the building, me leading with the pistol clasped in my bloodstained hand. One of Dale's men had a bottle of spray paint ready and proceeded to cover the lens of the camera as soon as we turned the corner.

This was it. No turning back. My heart beat out of my ears, but I felt steady, no fear. All I wanted was to see Becka safe, alive. All I wanted was to hold her tight, get her out of the warehouse, take her on that vacation to nowhere that she so desperately needed.

I closed my eyes and counted down—*three, two, one*. I opened my eyes and punched the master code into the lock. Behind me, two of Dale's men held a battering ram at the ready, and I half expected the light to blink red: *Denied*. But it didn't. The lock blinked green. Without hesitation, I swung the door open, my pistol leading the way as I stormed inside the building. A man began to stand from the folding chair only feet before me, a cup of coffee in his hand. He tried to form a word, but only got out, "Fuu—" before I shot him in his throat. Two more bullets struck the man, and the coffee cup shattered on the ground, steam dissipating in the air.

Taking an immediate left, I rushed down the vacant hallway. Ten men followed at my heels and the others went to the grow room door. The battering ram echoed loud down the hallway, booming against the metal door, as I neared the corner and turned.

Stopping before the break room, I counted down again—*three, two ... one*—and turned the handle, swinging the door back on its hinges. Just as the door opened, two large men not much older than teenagers came running out from the packaging and shipping room, pistols in hand.

Their eyes went large.

Bullets peppered them against the doorframe. Dale's shotgun boomed loud, some of the buckshot striking the refrigerator behind the men in metallic plunks. The coffee pot burst, sending shrapnel flying about the room.

I stepped over the dead men and into packaging and shipping. The bikers bottlenecked at the doorway, and someone dragged the dead men away by their ankles.

The room was empty.

The sound of muffled bullet shots came from the grow-room behind the walls.

I was at the door to the office, and this time I didn't count to three. I kicked the door open and stormed inside.

A half step in, I halted and stumbled.

She turned to me fast, her face alert and frightened. A gun raised in her hand.

"Becka …"

"Powers?"

We had each other locked in our guns' sights.

I raised my fist, indicating to Dale and his men to halt behind me.

"This her?" Dale asked at the doorway.

"Fuck off," I said, and kicked the door shut. "Secure the building," I shouted.

Becka was shaking.

I stared at her terrified face.

"Are you okay?"

"Yes …" She cut off, her eyes wide. "What happened to you? Are you bleeding?"

"It's not my blood. Are you okay?"

We both lowered our pistols.

"Powers, what the fuck are you doing here?" Her eyes were huge, watery. Some of the monitors behind her were black from the spray paint. "Are those bikers? Is that Dale?"

"Becka—are you safe?"

"Yes, yes. I'm safe. Whose blood is that?"

"Becka …" My grip tightened on my pistol, and I fought the urge to break eye contact to look at the gun in her hand.

And then I noticed something. I thought back to the photograph of Becka with the foul man gripping her shoulder. I studied her now, standing before me.

"Becka, where's that locket I gave you?"

"Why?"

"Where is it?"

She swallowed. "I don't know. Does that matter? I lost it somewhere. Powers—"

Before she could react, I jumped forward and grabbed her pistol in my left hand, twisting it out from her grip. Tucking it in my belt, I leveled my own gun back at her.

"How long, Becka? *How long* have you been working with them?"

"Powers, you're scaring me." Her eyes were huge, glassy, and her bottom lip quivered. She made a motion to approach me, embrace me, but I stepped back. "Was that Dale out there? Jesus Christ, Powers—why are the Barren Souls here?"

"Becka, explain this to me." I reached for the crumbled Polaroid in my pocket and handed it to her with extended fingers. She glanced at the photograph, then dropped it, letting it cascade to the floor. Her hands went to her mouth, and tears began to fall.

"You're wearing the locket I gave you in that picture, Becka. How long ago was that picture taken? How long have you been working with them?"

"I never …" She shook her head. "You aren't supposed to be here. You weren't supposed to make that delivery. Damn it, Powers! You shouldn't be messed up in all of this."

"Oh, I'm messed up in this pretty good right now. Keep talking."

"You don't understand. The bosses will be back any minute—it will be chaos when they arrive."

"Who, the twins? They're dead. They're all dead, Becka. And so is Nick. He's dead. Nick … is dead."

She looked up at me.

"Nick? How—*what happened?*"

"You go first."

She was trembling all over and cleared her throat before answering. "All right, man, all right. Just lower the gun. It's me you're talking to."

"I don't know who's who anymore."

"Okay ... I started working for them a few months ago. Maybe six. Nick ..." She paused, shaking her head. "He's not who you think he is."

"Yeah, I got that much. His name is Vitali—or was Vitali."

She nodded. "So you know."

"I know everything, Becka."

"No, Powers. No." She let out a sigh, wiping a stray tear. "No, man. You don't know a thing. Nick, or Vitali, came to the US from Russia when he was young, early twenties. He left behind a loving family, a mother and father, and a nineteen-year-old girlfriend. He promised all of these people new lives in the US once he had the means to provide. He promised his girlfriend marriage. He promised to take care of the baby in her womb ..."

And then it hit me.

"Oh, Jesus Christ."

Fragments of my conversation with Nick just a day ago flashed in my thoughts.

"Don't call her. Don't mention her name around the Russians ... "

He was protecting her. He was protecting his—

"You're ... Nick's daughter."

Becka cast her eyes to the ground and continued, "Let me tell you about Nick Grady. A few years passed with him in the US and me and my mother still in Russia. His father—my grandfather—passed away, and my grandmother got a visa to move to America. I'm told he visited once, still promising to move everyone over as soon as he could. He was working on it, he told my mom. He was working on setting up our future ... but he never delivered. One day, he vanished. Disappeared. Some angry men come to our home, demanding to know where he'd gone. They said he was back in Russia, but my mother swore that she hadn't seen him. They didn't believe her. They hit her, over and over. I was right there in the room. They weren't planning on killing her, I don't think. She managed to break free from their fists for a matter of moments, running to me, tears in her terrified eyes, blood running from her nose. The scene is fragmented in my memory, yet what I can remember will always be stuck in my mind, crystal clear. They reached for her … and she slipped. Simple as that. One of the men grabbed her, and her legs went out. She tumbled down the stairway beside her, her head slamming against the front door. As young as I was, I remember screaming—screaming for my mother. I was hollering when the men grabbed me, and a huge palm covered my mouth. I can still remember the stale smell of cigarettes on his hand. They had the decency, if you could call it that, to leave me a block away from a hospital, and told me to walk straight."

She paused. I cleared my throat to speak, but all I could get out was, "Shit."

She continued, "I was brought to America to live with my grandmother. She told me all about my father the criminal. Vitali, Nick, whatever you want to call him, met with her one time and one time only. He looked like a different man, she said, not her son. He gave her a large envelope of money and then disappeared. She managed to find him, though. It took years, but she searched until she finally saw him one day walking down the street. Yet she refused to confront him. Refused to speak to the man responsible for deserting his baby daughter and killing his fiancée. She prayed every day in front of her cross, her rosary beads draped in her fingers, praying for the demons tormenting his soul to leave her son be. But they never did. When I was a teenager she brought me to town, and we sat on a park bench. At nine a.m., my father's work truck parked in front of a coffee shop and she pointed her shaking finger. She said, 'There is the man who killed your mother. There is the man who left you for dead.'"

Becka paused to wipe away a tear.

"Jesus, Becka." I longed to grab her tight, hug away her pain. But I remained strong, vigilant. I didn't know this woman.

"So this is revenge," I said. "You killed him. You killed your father, to avenge your mother."

"No, no." Her hands covered her eyes. "He wasn't supposed to die, he wasn't. I swear. I …"

I still had the pistol aimed at her head. "Tell me what you did—what was your plan? You were working with the men who killed your mother, the organization responsible for beating her senseless and causing her to fall down the stairs."

"I had a plan ... I had a plan." The tears were really coming. "You're not supposed to be here, Powers. You weren't supposed to make that delivery. It was supposed to be Nick and Jim, like it's always been. The Russians, they thought I was working with them. I took that picture a month ago." She pointed to the Polaroid on the floor. "They were only going to use it if they thought Nick would fight back. They promised to let you and everyone else out of the operation. You could all be free. All they wanted was the business. They promised me that they wouldn't kill him. I was giving him the freedom he longed for—retirement."

"They lied to you. How could you believe them?"

"I didn't." Her eyes looked up at me, red and fierce. "I admit it, I wanted revenge. I wanted to see the man who had abandoned me suffer. When Nick discovered my identity, he promised me all sorts of things. The business, for one. Partial ownership over time."

"He was protecting you. He didn't want the Russians, or that cop, Frank, to know who you were."

"What does it matter? My father was a liar. He promised me the world and gave me a rotten apple. He's the devil, Powers. He's incapable of remorse. He feels no shame for his sins, no ownership over his actions. I was going to send them all to jail. All of them. The Russians. My father. You weren't supposed to make that delivery, man. I knew the Russians were going to meet Nick in Montana with the cocaine. All it would have taken was a single tip to the police, and they would have all been sent away."

"And then what?"

"And then ... the operation would be mine. I was going to bring you back when the dust settled, tell you everything."

"Bring me back? Well, guess what, I'm in charge now, Becka. The operation is mine." I pointed at my chest. "I'm the boss."

"What about those bikers? You working with *them*? They'll use this place to sell meth, crack, whatever."

"What difference does it make?" I shrugged. "Let them burn it down, for all I care. Maybe I'll burn the place to the ground myself before the night is through."

She looked at me, startled. "What happened to you, Powers?"

"What happened to *me*? You dare to fucking ask *what happened to me*? They're all dead—Jim, Darin—you killed them all."

"No. It wasn't supposed to happen like this."

"You killed your father, your only family."

She looked at the ground, her head slowly shaking, shoulders quivering.

"He—he wasn't supposed to die."

I continued, "Whatever demon plagued your father is manifest in your soul entirely. You got to destroy it, Becka. Otherwise, you're no better than this man you call the devil."

"Whatever good was inside me ..." Her chest fluttered as she inhaled, tears about to explode. "... died a long time ago, in Russia. All I've known since then is hardship. After my grandmother died, when I was eighteen, I took off. I traveled the streets with no money and barely any food. I spied on my father. Followed him around, from Dead show to Dead show. I became obsessed with him, obsessed with getting revenge. I'm ... there's nothing left inside me, Powers."

She looked up, stared down the barrel of my gun. My eyes welled, but I fought tears away.

"Do it, Powers. Do what I've been struggling to do."

"You need help, Becka. You can get help."

"Just fucking do it. Pull the trigger." She fell to her knees. "Burn this place to the ground. Destroy it all—light the fucking world on fire."

I swallowed. The barrel of my pistol aimed at her forehead, aimed at the spot I used to savor with kisses. Even from a distance, I could smell her sweet scent of vanilla.

Chapter 27

I got the grass seed and spreader. The bag said, "Guaranteed to grow on any surface."

All through the night I spread the seed.

When I finished, I wiped my dirty and battered hands on my jeans and took a seat at the base of the apple tree.

"Nick." I looked down at the fresh soil. Then I shook my head. Words weren't coming. There was nothing to say. I sat there until the morning sky turned a pale shade of blue.

My guess is that Nick went back to the house to die. The shoot-out wasn't supposed to happen. He thought that sacrificing his life would save his daughter's, and maybe mine.

But who knows.

After some time I stood.

"You're free now, brother."

Inside, I showered and changed. Nick had left a duffel bag out in the open on the kitchen table. I opened it and glanced inside.

Right on top of a large bundle of cash was a single piece of paper folded in three.

"Powers," was written on the top.

After reading it, I put the paper in my pocket. I grabbed the bottle of bourbon, all the money, a few meager belongings, and tossed them all on the passenger seat of my Buick.

As I drove away, I looked back one last time at the apple tree. In my head

I saw Nick dancing to his music as sprinkler water set the crops sparkling.

There was one more stop to make: the little office.

After wiping everything down with a rag as best as I could, I removed the wainscoting on top of the fake molding. I wore gloves as I turned the swivel lock of the solid metal safe and the little handle turned free. Inside was all the paperwork and stacks upon stacks of wrapped cash. More than I could imagine.

Back in the car, I tucked the money in the trunk and found a CD from the glove box.

I wasn't sure where I was going, but I had a few ideas. Somewhere warm sounded nice, but not Mexico or anywhere tropical. Nowhere out of the country. Maybe New Mexico or Arizona. Drinking a beer in a quiet adobe saloon out near the desert sounded all right.

The music played loud from the speakers as I rummaged through my bag for a cigar. I crumpled the note that Nick had given me, looking one last time at the words scrawled across the top.

"Take care of her," it said, and nothing more.

All of the windows were down. The warm air washed over me, filling my lungs, cleaning my sins. The burning cigar issued huge plumes of smoke out the window. The bright and colorful horizon loomed large, and I pressed down on the accelerator, driving fast toward the west.

Thank you for reading Whiskey Devils. *Please read on past the acknowledgments for a preview of Brandon Zenner's novel,* The Experiment of Dreams.

http://www.BrandonZenner.com
http://www.amazon.com/author/brandonzenner

Acknowledgments

In no particular order, the following people need a round of applause: John Graham, Hal Zenner, Tayberk Yolac, John Grandits, Aaron Kaiserman, and Kimberly Ito. You each contributed in a different way, and helped *Whiskey Devils* become a reality. I cannot thank you each enough.

From the Author

The first inkling of an idea for *Whiskey Devils* came about when I was twenty-one years old, maybe twenty-two. The skeleton concept came to me while driving cross-country with two of my friends, on a trip that I will never forget. That trip was so inspiring that I had to do it again a year later, but that time all by myself. Although *Whiskey Devils* was nothing more than a concept back then, I knew that I had the basis for a story. I clearly envisioned Evan Powers and Nick Grady, and their relationship and personalities did not change in all of the years before I finally wrote down their story. The first title back then was *Splintered Sunlight*, or just *Splintered*, but over time I began to see that title as too clearly a link to the Grateful Dead. When *Whiskey Devils* came to mind, it quickly took its place. In the end, I am pleased with the shape this decade-long novel took, and quite sad to see these characters that I am so fond of no longer dancing around in my mind. Evan and Nick, I hope you party on forever under the old apple tree.

If you enjoyed *Whiskey Devils*, the best way you can support the book is by taking a minute to leave a review on Amazon. I read and appreciate every review I receive. Here is a link to my Amazon page: http://www.amazon.com/author/brandonzenner

Visit http://www.BrandonZenner.com to learn more about past and future work, and join my email list to stay informed of everything I'm doing. As a thank you for joining my email list, you will receive the short story, "Helix Illuminated." What else do members of my email list receive? Well, this novel for one. All of my past followers were offered *Whiskey Devils* for free. You can also follow me on just about any social media outlet. Here's Facebook and Twitter:

https://www.facebook.com/brandon.zenner
https://twitter.com/SlapstickII

Thank you for reading *Whiskey Devils*, and please enjoy the preview of *The Experiment of Dreams* following this ramble.

All the best,
Brandon Zenner

Preview: The Experiment of Dreams

"The twists and turns of the plot will leave your head reeling and possibly questioning your own mental state for a moment. If you are looking for a tempestuous thriller, look no further as this book will surely fill the void."

   -The San Francisco Book Review

"A creative, sharply drawn thriller anchored by sturdy prose and a memorable hero."

   -Kirkus Reviews

"THE EXPERIMENT OF DREAMS is an absorbing study of how our perception of reality and imagination interact in the subconscious mind. The characters are true to life and the neuroscience is cutting edge yet understandable."

   -Indie Reader

Chapter 1

Ben cut across the empty parking lot of the Annapolis Foundation for Sleep Research, picking at the dried paste plastered to his scalp where the electrodes had been attached to his head the previous night. He enjoyed an odd sense of pleasure in removing the paste, like finding pockets of sand buried deep in his hair after a day at the beach.

It was shaping up to be a warm day, and as Ben neared his car, he flung his jacket over his shoulder, letting the sunlight warm his hospital-cold skin. Ben pulled his keys from his pocket, and a business card that Dr. Wright had given him slipped away and fluttered over the pavement on a light wind. Ben jumped to catch it, but it danced over the parking lot in a gust and was lost from sight.

Not a problem, he thought. Dr. Wright had given Ben the same business card three times already and had been urging him to call the doctor—whose name was on the card—for over a month now. He explained in detail how important it was for Ben to meet the man.

Ben fiddled with his keys, found the alarm button, and unlocked his car. He flicked away the dried paste left stuck to his fingers, brushed his hands off on his pant legs, and climbed into the driver's seat. The reflection gazing back at him in the rearview mirror was not flattering. Nights at that lackluster hospital made him feel so disheveled. His face was gaunt, his eyes were bleary and red, and the stubble on his face was in desperate need of a shave. He rubbed the side of his cheek, enjoying the sensation of the coarse hairs against his palm. The stubble gave off a silvery hue that reminded Ben that he was getting older. Even the hair on his head was now speckled with gray, like someone splattered a brush with drying white paint all over his head. He looked like his father, or rather how he remembered his father.

He turned his gaze from the mirror and put the car in drive.

Ben yearned for good coffee—not the sour crap they served in the hospital that tasted like the Styrofoam cups they served it in. The clock on the dashboard read 11:37. With any luck, he would be home in an hour—that is if he didn't stop along the way for coffee, and maybe some breakfast. And, of course, if the traffic around I-95 wasn't particularly unbearable. But the chances of the circle around Baltimore's Inner Harbor being anything but hellish during lunch hour were slim to none.

He hated that circle, loathed every car that sped along the pavement, cursed it with every breath in his body. As soon as he merged with the traffic, his life was put in imminent danger. Cars and trucks sped between lanes, weaving this way and that, coming dangerously close to hitting one another— inches from disaster. When Benjamin Walker moved to Baltimore, he named I-95 "Maryland's Inner Death Circle," and the name became more relevant with each passing day.

As bad as driving I-95 was, driving the streets of New York was not much better; Ben was glad his commute was no longer between Baltimore and New York City. Currently his drive between Baltimore and Annapolis took a little over an hour, and outside of the harbor, the drive was not bad at all. It was a good thing Dr. Wright left the city to take the job in Annapolis. His loyalty to the man might have eventually worn out. The commute was not worth the money, unless the doctor started paying substantially more, which of course, the hospitals would never agree to. Ben's fees and rates were set in contract, per test, and rarely—if ever—changed in the slightest. Compromise and negotiation were out of the question.

Nevertheless, Ben knew in his heart that he would miss the old doctor if he ever stopped participating in his tests and experiments. Not exactly like missing an old friend, though Stuart *was* an old friend, but more like missing a well-accustomed routine. Or like missing an old tree in the backyard after watching it grow over the years. The tree could be replaced, but it would never grow the same branches.

Lately, though, the work with Dr. Wright was good. The money was all right, and the sessions were regular enough that Ben considered it a real job. He could endure the old man's stale breath as he hovered over Ben's face attaching sensors and wires to his forehead and scalp. He could endure the sleep deprivation studies, the food abstention trials, the unknown medications presented in white Dixie cups, and the incredibly tedious paperwork and questionnaires he constantly had to fill out.

The biggest problem Ben dealt with over the last few years was not the pay or the long commute. It was the lack of anything new—anything exciting. The original tests, back when he was a teenager, were groundbreaking. At least they were to him. Over time, they became repetitive. The *same* sleep deprivation studies, the *same* food abstention trials, the *same* melatonin and B-12 supplements, over and over....

However, he could endure the boredom if the price was right. If the money kept rolling in, he would put up with it—and lately the money was rolling in.

Ben's curiosity was stirred, however, as they were wrapping up the sleep deprivation study earlier that morning.

Dr. Wright had paused, then said, "Ben, I have something for you. I'm not sure how to do this, so I'm just going to go ahead and do it." The tall doctor scratched the light fuzz on the side of his hairless head, wrinkling his trimmed mustache. "I want our working relationship to stay as professional as always."

"Sure, Stuart, so do I. What's up?"

"Here." He handed Ben a white envelope. "There's five hundred dollars in there."

"Wait, is this all I'm getting? This study lasted over a month, I'm contracted—"

"Your check for the study is in the mail. This is a little something extra, a bonus. We appreciate your years of work at the hospital. This is just a little something to show our gratitude."

Ben thumbed open the envelope. *Our gratitude?* Five crisp, one-hundred-dollar bills were stacked inside, all facing the same direction. The money smelled new—starchy and fresh. Ben scratched his head. "Is this your way of firing me, like a pension or something?"

"No, no, Ben." The doctor shook his head. "Nothing of the sort. Not long ago we received some private funding at the hospital from some very generous donors. These individuals are following your work and dedication to the hospital; in return, these donors would like to show their appreciation by giving you a bonus. That's all there is to it. Just a bonus."

Each payment Ben had ever received over the many years working with Dr. Stuart Wright came in the form of a check written out to the exact amount. Ben even declared the earnings on his income tax, on a 1099-MISC form. Cash was never an option, never mentioned. Neither was a bonus. Hospitals do not run like that. Doctors get bonuses, but test subjects do not.

"This is cash, Stuart."

"I know it is." Dr. Wright's mustache moved with his sigh. "I think you can understand why we need to keep this … to ourselves. These are *private* investors, Ben, and it's just a bonus." He patted Ben on the shoulder. "We've been working together for a long time now, and you deserve a few extra dollars every once in a while. Don't think so hard; you'll give yourself a migraine. Just say 'thank you,' and take the cash." He smiled, wrinkling the furrows on his bald forehead.

Private investors rolled around Ben's head. He stared at the money—cash money, five hundred dollars, tax free. Ben had worked in the bar business for most of his life; even owned a small place in upstate New York that did quite well while it was open. It wasn't unusual for a few dollars here and there to slip through the cracks and not get reported to the IRS. This was normal in the bar scene. But from a doctor, from a hospital? Perhaps the less he knew the better. He folded the envelope and tucked it inside his jacket pocket.

"Tell them 'thank you.'"

"I will, Ben. I will."

This conversation played over in Ben's mind as he eyed his jacket lying on the passenger seat, where the five hundred dollars were folded inside. He shook his head.

Strange, he thought.

Rent money, he assured himself.

Ben survived "Maryland's Inner Death Circle," certain that several of the other drivers were trying to kill him, and found a space to park less than two blocks from his door. Walking past a flower-store delivery van that lately always seemed to be parked around his block, he arrived at the entryway of the four-unit apartment building—an old, converted row house that he called home.

At the top of the staircase on the second floor were two apartments with their front doors mirroring each other on opposite sides of a small landing. Ben's apartment was the door to the left. He unlocked the deadbolt, turned the handle, and hurried inside, happy to be back in his own space with his own bed and comfortable couch. The apartment was not much to look at—just a narrow one-bedroom flat—but the interior had a bit of character. The living room wall opposite the front door was solid brick and ran the length of the room. It was open to the kitchen and a dining-room nook where Ben stored unopened boxes from when he first moved into the apartment. Ben liked the brick wall, liked it very much. It probably drove the rent up an extra hundred dollars a month, but he didn't care. It gave the place a touch of personality.

Ben tossed his keys on the kitchen counter, grabbed the bottle of dish soap from the sink, and walked straight to the bathroom. He changed out of his hospital clothing, burying the dirty garments deep in the hamper. Anything he wore in hospitals during trials and tests absorbed that antiseptic hospital stench—that sterile smell that reminded Ben of the color white—and lingered on his skin for hours after.

A hot shower removed more of the electrode-crust plastered in Ben's hair and scalp, but whatever the stuff was that the doctor used, it never cleaned off completely with soap and water. After years of trials, Ben found that dish soap worked the best. Now clean and fresh—the hospital smell scrubbed from his skin—Ben put on his old well-worn robe and collapsed on the couch.

His body was sore, his mind exhausted. He needed a few hours of rest before heading to his shift at the bar. He wished he had never agreed to work that night, but filling in shifts was why the bar hired him. Ben was obliged to work when an employee was sick or went on vacation, or when someone just wanted the night off. A few shifts a week always popped up.

It was times like these—these lazy afternoons—that Ben wished he had cable TV. The old square box on the shelf wasn't even plugged in. Why he didn't just get rid of the thing, he didn't know. Of course, he could plug it in, look for the antenna in one of the boxes in the dining room, and maybe pick up a few channels, but there was nothing on TV worth watching. Besides, he wasn't even sure if TVs still used those old-fashioned antennas. Instead, he just sat there, gazing at the stack of books on the coffee table, debating whether he was too tired to read anything at all. The only books on the coffee table were philosophy—Nietzsche, and the like—all books that he started reading at some point or another and never finished. In his current frame of mind, he couldn't handle philosophy.

He looked up from the books, his gaze wandering, until the solitary painting hanging by the front door stole his attention. It was the only painting created by his beloved wife Emily that he still owned. It was the only thing remaining from his old life in upstate New York.

It was a small painting, about a foot and a half square.

The swirls of paint were still vibrant, still brilliant. It was a painting of the cabin in the woods, the cabin they hiked past dozens of times. A small wooden building hidden among the towering pines. A whisper of smoke trailed from the chimney, hinting of the cabin's warm and cozy interior, sheltered from the blustery air. Snow covered the ground in half-melted patches, with stale, dead grass poking out from beneath. Clouds soared in the blue sky, illuminated by swirls of creamy zinc and titanium white paint. The sun was barely visible in the corner, brought to life by yellow and orange swirls, twisting and turning with various shades of red. This painting, out of the many paintings in Emily's studio—the landscapes, still lifes, and portraits— had always been his favorite. The scene was realistic in detail, yet she used her own flair of artistic imagery to turn it into a surrealistic figment of her imagination. The sky swirled in shades of blue and purple never found in nature, yet her artistic ability was subtle enough to make these irregularities easy to overlook at first glance. It was not until you spent time absorbing the painting in full that the irregularities became apparent to see. It was genius.

At least it was to Ben.

This was the only painting he had taken from her studio. He left the others neatly stacked in the corner of her paint-flecked room, exactly where Emily had last touched them.

After she died, Ben could not be around her things—not even the house they lived in. He could not sleep in the bed they'd shared for the eight years of their marriage, side by side. He couldn't look at her clothes, or her shoes— the leather boots she'd just polished and left out to dry—or her toothbrush balanced on the corner of the sink. He couldn't look at her watch with its coiled black-leather strap, sitting on the bedside table where she had last taken it off.

When he stepped into that house for the first time all alone, straight from the hospital, he was still wearing the same clothes from the night before, speckled with blood—her blood. The quiet and stillness all around him was maddening. It took a considerable amount of strength just to step away from the front door. He wanted to be outside, to run as far away as possible. These things, *her* things, were causes of great pain—not relief, not comfort, nor gentle remembrance, just pain.

She was everywhere in that house. She was still in her studio, standing in front of her easel with her back facing him. Her image on the large plate-glass windows reflected the focused concentration of her creased brow as she applied a stroke of color with her brush. He saw her applying her makeup in front of the bathroom sink, her face an inch away from the mirror. He smelled her in the almond-scented shampoo and the little jasmine-scented bars of soap with the Chinese writing on the packaging. Everything in his home reminded him of her. Emily had seeped into the very walls, fibers, and structure of their home. It was impossible that she was gone, absolutely impossible—she couldn't be. She was everywhere in that house, around every corner, and in every room.

But she wasn't there. She was gone.

Taken from him like all the rest.

A simple accident. A stupid fight at the bar. Two drunken patrons fighting over something. Anything. Nothing. Sports, maybe. A girl, perhaps ... it didn't matter. Words were spoken and punches were thrown. By the time Ben heard the commotion and ran out from the kitchen, it was over. Stunned customers were circling about. The two men stood slack-jawed and in shock, all their anger deflated. Emily lay on the ground bleeding, the knife by her side. She had tried to stop the fight, tried to get between the two men.

That was it, an accident. No sickness, no long hospitalization. She was healthy and vibrant one moment, dead the next.

Ben left New York, left their old home and sold it all, leaving everything behind but for one thing: the painting of the cabin in the woods.

As time passed, his decision to abandon Emily's possessions caused countless nights of regret and anguish. Those items, however painful they were at the time, would have been most welcome as the years went by and the reality of her being gone truly sank in. The longing to possess anything and everything of hers became an obsession, a comforting need, and an endless source of torment and sorrow. How could he have left everything? Why? He had to smell her, hold her, squeeze one of her shirts in his hands, smother it against his face. Breathe in lungfuls of her fragrant scent lingering on one of her silk shirts—but it was all gone. Ben called the agent who sold the house and contacted the current owners in an attempt to track down any of the paintings left behind, but to no avail. All of Emily's possessions were gone, and all Ben had left were his memories.

These thoughts and needs raced through his mind in endless waves of guilt as he stared into the swirls of paint in the sky above the cabin in the woods. Feelings pierced his mind like sharp blades, slashing away without consequence, sinking their cold metal teeth deep into the flesh of his brain.

The painting brought back memories both beautiful and horrid. He saw his wife painting, her reflection in the plate-glass window, her forehead furrowed in concentration, paint smeared and dotted all over her hands, forearms, and face. He stood in the doorway, just looking, not wanting Emily to see him looking at her. Just enjoying the pleasure of watching her work, doing the thing that made her most happy ... and *that*, seeing her smile, was what made him happy ... so happy ....

Ben got up from the couch. The bottle of Jameson on the counter was calling his name. The thought of a drink made his stomach rumble and his mind swirl, but he could not let the rest of the day be consumed by dwelling on the past. It was too easy to spend hours staring at the painting while drinking to oblivion, as if the painting held some great divinity that he desired—the answers he needed, and the cure for the pain he both longed for and resented.

He licked his lips. His head throbbed. The yearning for a stiff drink stung at his mind, made his mouth salivate. His throat had a dryness only alcohol could soothe. A twinge of pleasure was released at the very thought of taking a sip of whiskey—a foresight into the relief the alcohol would have on his body and mind.

He turned away from the bottle and went to the bedroom, setting the alarm. Sleeping in the middle of the day was tough, but he needed some rest before work. Three hours should do it. He grabbed his blindfold from the bedside table and accidentally brushed off the business card hiding beneath. Bending over, he retrieved the card from the floor, noisily exerting himself from the strain. Printed across the center of the card was the name, "*Dr. Peter Wulfric*" followed by a telephone number underneath. Dr. Wright had emphasized to Ben that Dr. Wulfric was working on a very exciting project and was looking for a client. He paid very well. Ben had put the card in his pocket and then on the bedside table, then forgot all about it. The same went for the other two.

Then Dr. Peter Wulfric had called him.

The man was happy and pleasant and urged Ben to meet with him. Ben shied away, telling the doctor, '*I can't get out of town … I've got a lot on my plate right now.*' Dr. Wulfric volunteered to travel to him, to Baltimore, just so they could talk—a quick lunch. Perhaps it was intrigue, or perhaps curiosity when Ben asked what hospital the doctor worked for and the doctor said, '*We can discuss that when we talk face-to-face,*' that made Ben's interest grow. He conceded to a meeting. Dr. Peter Wulfric was coming to Fells Point in two days, and hopefully he would pick up the lunch tab.

Ben tossed the card back on the bedside table and pulled the covers up to his chin. The blindfold was fastened tightly over his eyes, shielding away the intense rays of sunlight penetrating through the blinds. He took a deep breath and relaxed his mind. Sleep was not going to come easily.

Thoughts of the painting along with visions of Emily flashed in his mind: her dark curly hair bouncing on her shoulders as she laughed, paint on her face, cheeks, and hair. He saw his own finger dip into a pool of dark blue paint from the palette and watched his finger move to smear her nose. She shrieked with laughter, grabbed at his palm and fell backward. She was laughing too hard to resist, and his finger found her nose, rubbing it all over with the oily blue paint.

She shrieked, *'Stop, Ben!'*

He heard his own laughter as they kissed. She grabbed him close, not letting him go, holding him by the ears and smearing her paint-covered nose all over his face.

He saw this as it happened, in that paint-speckled studio of hers. He heard the laughter and felt the warmth of love in his heart. His blindfold grew warm with the onset of tears.

Continue reading: http://amzn.to/WbpCM0